VISION OF LOVE

VISION OF LOVE

LINKED ACROSS TIME

DAWN BROWER

For Barbara J. Richards
*Your larger than life personality, no nonsense attitude,
and kind heart will always be remembered. Having you
for a friend was one of my greatest blessings and
privileges.*
*Thank you for being a part of my life. The world will not
be the same without you in it. You will forever be missed
by many, me included.*

CONTENTS

TEMPTING AN AMERICAN PRINCESS

EXCERPT: CHARMING HER ROGUE

CHAPTER ONE

May 4, 1951

 he weather had been far better than Lady Anya Montgomery could have hoped for. In a few short hours, the Festival of Britain would start, and she had to ensure everything went off without a hitch. Her very livelihood might depend upon it. All right, that was perhaps an exaggeration. Thanks to her father, the Earl of Parkdale, she was independently wealthy, but that didn't mean she had no goals or ambition. She had been working at the British Film Institute for almost a year as an assistant to one of the women in charge. Anya had also taken several courses at the BFI Film Academy.

One day, she hoped to direct and produce her own films...

She rushed into the office with a cup of coffee for her boss. Lady Vivian Kendall was on the phone, sitting on a corner of her desk. She glanced at Anya and waved her in. She had her dark hair plaited and woven into a bun at the nape of her neck. Her cobalt, satin, jacquard dress was exquisite, a full circle skirt and black petticoats underneath giving it a nice flare. She also had a black belt, T-strap heels, and gloves. Anya felt dowdy in comparison in her simple red skirt and white blouse, and plain black Mary Jane's. She'd wanted to be as comfortable as possible for the long day ahead of her. Clearly, Lady Vivian didn't know the meaning of comfort. Not in the practical sense anyway.

"See that it's done," Lady Vivian said into the phone. "I won't accept excuses. You know how important this festival is, and we cannot afford to have anything go wrong. It's already been politicized more than it should be. This is supposed to be a celebration of all things British." She sighed. "This is *needed*. The war was long and brutal and something good, like this event, will be fun will benefit everyone."

Anya didn't want to know who she was talking

to. They must have imparted some awful news, and she hoped it wouldn't delay anything in the festival. They had all worked so hard to see it come to fruition. She stared down at her hand, and the opal ring her grandmother had given her. A floral leaf design had been woven on the sides of the silver metal and encircled the round opal at the top. When her grandmother had given it to her, she'd told her to follow her heart. She had kept that advice in mind when she'd taken the position at the British Film Institute.

"All right," Lady Vivian said. Her voice filled with frustration. "Keep me updated. I'll be down at the South Bank site soon." She placed the phone on the receiver and turned her attention to Anya. "Please tell me that is coffee," she said.

"It is," Anya answered and handed her a cup. "I thought you might need some. I could get tea…"

Lady Vivian shook her head. "No, coffee is perfect. My mum is American and prefers it, so I've developed an appreciation for both coffee and tea." She smiled. "Are you ready for an exhausting but exciting day?"

"I am." Anya smiled at her. "I am going to the Telekinema soon. I finished everything here. Is there anything you need me to do before I leave?"

She shook her head. "No. I'm leaving after I finish this coffee. I'll see you there, and please, have Ben find me immediately. I want to discuss the first set of films we are going to show in the cinema. There are a few small changes that need to be made."

"All right." Anya nodded. What changes? They had been discussing everything in detail for months, and the buildings weren't exactly erected overnight. "I'll let him know when I arrive at the Telekinema. He should be setting up the first film by now. I trust that one isn't going to be changed."

"It's not," Lady Vivian confirmed. "Some of the later ones today will be shuffled around. We will still have the same line up, but they are going to be screened in a different order and different days. Unfortunately, the programs already printed cannot be changed. We will make sure to post them on the marquee so the audience is aware of the modifications."

Anya didn't have much to add, so she nodded and turned to leave. As she reached the door, Lady Vivian called to her. "Wait."

"Yes?" Anya asked.

"Did you finish that memo I asked you to write?"

"Of course. Did you want to review it before it's sent out?" She should have considered Lady Vivian might want to do that. Her boss could be a bit controlling at times. She wanted to examine everything that went out in her name or she had a hand in executing.

"Yes," she replied as she stared at a document on her desk. "Bring it to me before you leave. If there are any changes, I'll make notes on it. Either way, I'd like it sent out tomorrow first thing to all the departments."

Anya went to her desk and pulled the memo out of a stack of typed pages. Most of them had to be put in envelopes and mailed out. They still required Lady Vivian's signature though, and she wouldn't want to handle those until she was certain the festival was running smoothly. The letters were not high priority, regardless. With the memo in hand, she returned to the office. "Here it is," she told Lady Vivian.

"Fabulous," she said. "Set it there on my desk."

"Is there anything else?"

"No." Lady Vivian glanced up and smiled at her. "Go try and enjoy yourself and help me make this day the best for all of Britain."

"I'll do my best," Anya told her. She left Lady Vivian's office, for good this time, and headed out of the building. Her heart beat fast inside her chest. She didn't know why, but it seemed like something profound might happen to her. It was probably a silly feeling, but it unsettled her a little bit.

She shook the feeling away as best she could and walked out of the building. If she hurried, she could catch the next bus to South Bank. Anya rushed down the street and stopped near a local bus stop. She didn't have long to wait until a red double-decker pulled to a stop in front of her. After the doors swung open, she stepped inside and found a seat. It wouldn't be long until she reached the Telekinema and she'd be able to learn firsthand everything involved in showing films to hundreds of people at a time.

ANYA STARED out the window as the bus rolled across some of London's prominent streets. The trek from Lady Vivian's building to the South Bank of the river Thames was a short one. Anya's flat was located between both. Her parents would have preferred she stayed home, but traveling from Mayfair could be tedious at times, and she didn't particularly wish to purchase an automobile yet. Not when she could walk to most places or take a bus for the longer treks. Perhaps she was an odd society lady in that she didn't flaunt her wealth. She tried to avoid using her title whenever possible. Lady Vivian was aware of who Anya's parents were but respected her wishes to drop the lady part of her title. She only used it when she was attending a high society function and it was expected.

The bus came to a stop near the river. She stood to exit, along with several other people. There were lines already at the gate. At least it wouldn't be a total failure like some people expected. Lady Vivian would be glad to see the crowds. The festival was meant to be celebrated all through the country, but the main festivities were held at the South Bank location. A few different areas presented art, music, science, and film. Even the architecture was designed specifically for the event. No expense had been spared.

Anya went to a back entrance for those that were working the festival. She showed her credentials to the guard, and he let her pass through, straight to the British Film Institute's pride and joy of the festival. The Telekinema was a four hundred seat state of the art cinema that was completely operated by the British Film Institute. They had plans to screen films, television shows, and even three-dimensional films. This was the first time many of the visitors would ever see any televised pictures, and Anya was excited to bring that to the masses. One day it might become the norm for a large-scale event such as the Festival of Britain.

She wandered to the area where the projector was being set up to show some of the films. Ben stood nearby, talking to one of the ushers that would be working during the showcase. "Tell the rest of the men to stand at the back of the theater once the film starts. No one likes it when their view is disrupted unnecessarily. Your job is to watch the audience and ensure no one is troublesome. Any issues and they are to be expelled from the theater without preamble. Do you understand?"

The young man nodded. "I'll relay the message."

"Good," Ben said. "We open in an hour. Go prepare everyone."

The festival itself would open to the public in mere minutes. The Telekinema was locked down tight until it officially opened. Lady Vivian would have to be there to give her speeches out front and at the ribbon cutting ceremony shortly after that. Then the public could purchase admittance to the theater and see the movies scheduled for the day.

When the young usher wandered off, Anya went

over to Ben and placed a hand on his shoulder. He jumped. "Christ, Anya, are you trying to make me die young of a heart attack?"

"Sorry," she apologized. "I didn't mean to startle you. Lady Vivian asked me to give you a message."

"It's fine," he said. "I'm naturally jumpy today. What did the boss say?"

Anya relayed the message, and he made notes in his booklet. "All right, I'll take care of it. Shouldn't she be here already?"

"There were a few last minute items she had to see to before she left. She'll be here in time for the big event."

He didn't appear happy. Maybe this was aging him prematurely. Ben wasn't that much older than her. He had at least five years to her twenty-one, but he looked even older than Lady Vivian who would celebrate her thirty fourth birthday in a few months. Ben had dark spots under his eyes, and his skin almost seemed paler than normal. His blond hair probably didn't help. It was so light it almost appeared white. He ran his hand through those fair locks, leaving a rumpled mess in its wake. "This is complete chaos."

Anya glanced around her but didn't see it the same way he did. "It looks like a well-oiled machine to me. Everyone is doing their assigned tasks, and when it is time to open the doors it'll go smoothly."

"From your lips to…" he said and glanced up to the ceiling

"…his ears."

"I doubt we need his approval today." She wasn't particularly religious. Anya didn't want to believe in a higher power or fate. She wanted to make her own way in the world and liked to think she made the decisions, not some all-powerful entity.

"I'll take any support," he said simply. "We need this to go well."

He wasn't wrong. "It will be fine." Her tone wasn't too enthusiastic, but she didn't know what else to say to him. She wanted to wander around and explore everything. The last thing she needed was to be his one-woman support system.

"I…" His voice trailed off as something caught his attention. "Stop," he yelled. "What do you think you're doing?" His tone turned frantic and he started to wave his hands. He stepped forward; probably to stop the person he was yelling at from doing whatever he thought was wrong.

Anya didn't really care, but it interested in a weird way. She sighed and started to walk away, but at the last minute she turned to glance behind her.

Someone was carrying a very large projection box, and his or her vision seemed to be hampered by it. Ben continued to flail his hands frantically. The person carrying the box tripped over a wire and the box went flying forward. Anya tried to duck out of the way, but it didn't help. The box landed on top of her, knocking her to the floor. Her head bounced several times against the floor, and the room began to spin then went completely dark, and any thought she might have had faded away into that void.

*A*nya's head hurt. Tiny hammers happily pounded against her skull in thousands of different places, but they seemed particularly focused on her forehead above her eyes. She was afraid to open her eyelids for fear it would make her pain worsen somehow. What happened to her? She couldn't remember how she'd hurt herself, and she wasn't certain she wanted to.

Bright light floated above, forcing her to block it with her arm. She turned her head until her eyes, still closed, were against the juncture of her bent arm. "Who turned on the bloody lights?" she grumbled out the words.

"It's time to wake up, Miss Ana," a woman said. "The duke and duchess will be down for breakfast soon, and your father expects you to act like a proper lady."

"I am a proper lady," she corrected her. She even had that as part of her formal title if she chose to use it. "I don't feel well. Please give my regrets." Anya nestled down into the blankets and managed to bury herself underneath them. Once there, the words the woman had said penetrated her addled brain. "What duke and duchess?" More importantly, who the hell was this woman, and why did she feel comfortable barging into Anya's bedchamber? Something wasn't right.

Carefully, she pulled the blanket down and cautiously opened one eye. The woman wore a dull gray dress that covered every inch of her. It was... archaic. Anya couldn't think of a better word to describe her. "Who are you?"

"Now, now, Miss Ana," she chastised her while wagging a finger. "Pretending an illness will not help you out of your situation. You know your responsibilities." She held up a navy blue dress, a little fancier than her dull gray one, but old fashioned, nonetheless. "Here is your day dress. After breakfast, you are to prepare to travel to the boatyard. You have a long journey ahead of you, and it'll take a while until you reach Germany."

Did she call her Ana? Somehow, she'd missed that the first time. Did she think Anya was someone else? She nibbled on her bottom lip, confused about everything. Her head still throbbed something fierce. There was only one way to handle the situation— roll with it for now. Slowly, she pulled herself to a sitting position. Even her pajamas were odd. She would have to call her parents and find out why they wanted her to visit with this duke and duchess. Anya didn't know this woman and couldn't help mistrusting her. She wrinkled her nose at the dress. "Do I really have to wear that?"

"What is wrong with it?" The woman stared at it and frowned. Her hair was a dull brown streaked with white, and her eyes were a steely gray that unnerved Anya. "It's made from the finest silk. You picked out the pattern yourself."

She'd done no such thing, but there was no point arguing with the woman. Instead, she sighed and held out her hand. "Fine. Give it to me and I'll put it on."

"Don't you require assistance?"

"I can manage on my own. I've been dressing myself for years now." This woman was clearly old-school. People didn't have maids anymore.

"Maybe you are feeling ill," the woman said and

came to her side. She placed one of her hands on her head. "You don't feel warm."

"Please do not touch me," Anya said through gritted teeth. She snatched the dress from the woman and stood. "Now, kindly leave so I may dress."

"Hmmph," she said disgruntled. "You're in a fine mood today. Maybe if you were not up half the night doing God knows what you'd be well rested instead of acting like a harpy in the morning. Don't dawdle. The duke and duchess will not wait on someone like you to make an appearance." With those words, she stomped out of the room.

What had she meant? She was Lady Anya Montgomery, and no one had ever talked to her like that. She stripped off her pajamas and looked in the dresser for a bra, but couldn't find anything but a silk tank top. It would have to do. The dress wasn't that formfitting, and it should be all right for the time being. Anya slid it on and then stared at the blue dress. It had buttons up the back. She groaned. She undid two and slid it over her head. Luckily, her head fit through it, and then she struggled to get the other two buttoned. If she came down even remotely half-dressed, that horrid woman would have a reason to chastise her.

She blew out a breath and sighed. Anya still had no idea where she was, but she'd find out soon enough. She sat down at the vanity and picked up a brush. As she started to run it through her tangled hair, she nearly screamed. Not from the pain that still permeated her skull, but the reflection in the mirror. That wasn't her. Slowly, she lifted her hand and touched her face. She pressed her fingers into her cheekbones several times. Her nails left tiny half-moon shaped indents in their wake. Still she kept pressing...hoping...praying her fears would not be realized. This couldn't be real. This was a nightmare...one she failed to wake fully from.

The woman had called her Ana, not Anya. The name was similar enough she'd dismissed it, but what if she was no longer Anya, but this Ana person. That would explain everything that had confused her. It, however, did not explain how she'd woken up in another woman's body. It was a bad movie plot, and she didn't like one second of it. She wanted to close her eyes and start the entire day over again. That wasn't possible though.

Perhaps it was... She could lie back down and close her eyes; then when she opened them again, it would all be over. No more body-switch and mean old maid to torment her. Shouldn't she at least try it?

Anya rushed over to the bed and climbed back in. She tossed the covers over her head and snapped her eyelids shut.

Nothing.

Her brain wouldn't stop thinking, and sleep proved to be impossible. She had to face reality: this nightmare was indeed real. She laid there for several seconds in disbelief, but the facts remained the same. Somehow, she would have to stumble her way through this Ana's life and not mess up. That would be as impossible as the situation she currently found herself in...

This duke and duchess, whoever they were, expected someone named Ana to come downstairs. If she failed to impersonate this other woman, what would they do to her? She had to find out as much information as possible without giving herself away. She'd already bumbled by throwing the maid out of the room.

Anya took a deep breath and brushed her hair. Then twisted it into a braid and wound it into a bun at the nape at her neck. It wasn't elegant, but at least it sort of matched the style of the gown—old-fashioned, and quite out of date, at least for Anya... With that done, she located shoes and left the room, praying with each step that she managed to locate the dining room without incident...

LUCK WAS ON HER SIDE... She was familiar with the style of townhouse and locating the breakfast nook proved easy enough. Anya walked into the room and found, what she presumed to be, a family of four. A man, the duke probably, sat at the head of the table, with his wife next to him along with a young lady around sixteen and a boy half her age.

The lady, presumably the duchess, glanced up at her and said, "Miss Ana." She had golden brown hair and striking blue eyes. "Please join us." She gestured toward a seat next to the young boy. "Mathias," she chastised. "Quit playing with your oatmeal and eat it."

Anya held back a grin and sat next to the boy. She leaned down and whispered, "I don't care for oatmeal either."

He glanced up at her and frowned. He had silvery blue eyes that were breathtaking. The boy tilted his head to the side as he studied her, then said, "Who are you?"

She swallowed hard, unnerved by his question.

How did she answer that? Did he mean it literally, and if so, did that mean he realized she wasn't really who they all believed her to be. She didn't get a chance to answer him as a servant set a plate before her filled with scrambled eggs, bacon, and toast. "Thank you," she said. She held back a groan. Her head still hurt and now her stomach was queasy on top of it. She glanced up and gasped as she met the young lady's gaze. Across the room, she hadn't realized… "Lady Vivian," she said carefully. It couldn't be…

"Yes," Lady Vivian said, perplexed. "What is it?"

The last time Anya recalled seeing her was in the office at the British Film Institute. She was much older than this waif of a girl in front of her. She was not only in another's body; she'd somehow fallen back in time. What was she supposed to say? She couldn't very well say, *"Oh, you are not the Lady Vivian I'm acquainted with."* Technically, it was the same person, only a younger version. One, she hadn't met, should never have met… Hell, Anya hadn't even been born yet. At least she thought so… She wasn't certain what year it was, and she guessed at it from the looks of Lady Vivian. She frowned.

"Nothing," she mumbled. "My apologies. I have

the worst head pain, and it's making it difficult to hold a thought."

"You poor dear," the duchess said. "Why didn't you say something. I'll have someone bring you something for that." She snapped her fingers at a nearby servant, and he wandered off. He came back a few moments later with two aspirin, and Anya took them off the platter. She swallowed them without thinking, glad to have something for her head pain.

The duke picked up a paper and opened it up. Anya wanted to gasp again, but held it in by sheer will. The headlines concerned her and gave her a lot to consider. Germany was front and center on the paper. It was September 1933, and their persecution of the Jewish community had already begun. She swallowed hard. It answered some of her questions... Like, she had been born, but she was no more than three years old. She didn't know what to do or how to act. None of it made any kind of sense.

"Ida said she has all your bags packed," the duchess began. Anya had to try to recall her name. She knew it... If only her head didn't hurt so much. "Are you prepared for the lengthy journey?"

More importantly, who was Ida? The answer clicked...the old woman...the maid. "I believe so."

Anya didn't have any other answer for…Brianne. Vivian's mother's name was Brianne. Though it wouldn't be right to use it. She should say *Your Grace* and follow proper etiquette. "She informed me when she woke me…" Wait…she'd also said she was traveling to Germany. Anya inwardly cursed. That was the last place she wanted to be in 1933. The war had been terrible and she had no desire to experience the worst of it firsthand, and in one of the most horrendous places of its culmination.

"She's efficient," the duchess said and smiled. "It has been a pleasure having you here. Your father was kind to assist us when we traveled to New York a couple years ago. As you know, my family lives in South Carolina and has a house in New York." She did know that…though she had forgotten. "Vivian…" She gave her daughter a wary glance. "…got lost in Central Park. Without your father's aid, we may never have located her."

Hmmm. That was interesting. Lady Vivian was a bit of a hellion. It didn't resemble the woman that Anya had come to know. If she ever returned to her own body and time, she might have to ask Lady Vivian what she'd done alone in Central Park at the age of fourteen. "My father was happy to help." She

21

hoped that was the truth. Anya had no idea who her "father" was.

"Edward Wegner is a good man. I hope he enjoys his new post with the Ambassador in Germany." The duke folded his paper and set it aside. "Though, I'm not certain he'll be there long if the current climate is anything to go by." The duke sighed. "The Great War was horrible, and no one wants to relive that, but I fear we may be heading toward another war."

The duke didn't know how right he was. Anya swallowed hard and tried to eat. She speared her eggs with a fork and shoved a bite into her mouth. No one would expect her to say much while she chewed.

"Don't scare her, Julian," the duchess said. "She is already dealing with a lot." She smiled at her. "You've been to Germany though. Isn't it lovely...what you've seen, anyway?" There was something unidentifiable in the duchess's voice. Had she been to Germany? If Anya remembered correctly, the duke had been a spy during the first world war. He had probably been to Germany, but the duchess was American. She'd undoubtedly stayed safe at home.

Anya swallowed the eggs, and it hurt as they traveled down her throat. She nodded. "Yes." One word answers were good, right?

"I understand you're engaged," the duke said.

"I am?" That shouldn't have come out as a question. Why was she going to Germany then?

The duchess laughed. "You might want to consider rethinking your relationship if you're not certain. Your father said he's in the German Army...a high-ranking officer."

What was this Ana thinking? Did she believe in the Nazi cause? "I'm certain it is the right decision to make." At least, she hopes so. Perhaps Ana loved the man. She'd hate to ruin her relationship.

"Well," the duchess said. "Either way, you have your whole life ahead of you. Some decisions cannot be so easily undone, and loving the man you marry should not be a difficult one."

"I agree," Anya said, and she did. If and when she married, she planned on loving the man to distraction. "If you will excuse me, I'd like to freshen up before I have to leave."

"Of course," the duchess said. "If I do not see you before you leave, have a safe trip."

With those words, Anya left the room. She still didn't know much, but she'd found out enough to give her pause. This was *not* good...not at all...

CHAPTER THREE

October 1933

nya stared out the window of the car as it took her from the train station to the location of the temporary American Embassy. She had no concept of time. At least not in the sense she definitely was not where she belonged. Everyone believed her to be Anastasia Wegner, daughter to a staff member of Ambassador William Dodd.

As far as she could tell, she had nothing in common with Anastasia. She had no ambition and was a dutiful daughter. Had even agreed to an engagement to a German officer. Bile rose in her throat at the idea of marrying a Nazi. She couldn't do it. There was one thing similar to her time, and just one: the opal ring on her ring finger. It was identical to the one her grandmother had gifted her...down to the floral leaf design in the silver metal and round opal.

She hadn't noticed it at first. With everything she'd awoken to and how much her head hurt, she'd overlooked the one piece of jewelry

she...Ana had been wearing. It could be a coincidence, but she didn't think it was. It was Ana's engagement ring. Anya wanted to take it off her finger and fling it somewhere it wouldn't ever be located. She couldn't do that though. Dutiful Ana wouldn't, and therefore Anya had to restrain her urges.

She blew out a breath and closed her eyes. They would be at the embassy soon, and she'd have to meet Ana's father. The little she'd learned about him hadn't left her with a good feeling. He might have done the Duke and Duchess of Weston a good turn, but he seemed to rule his house in a less than kind manner. She would have to hold back from speaking her mind. Saying the wrong thing could very well earn her a slap in the face.

Traveling with Ida had taught her that.

After they had left the Duke and Duchess's home Ida had turned into a different woman. Well, that wasn't true exactly. What had changed is how she believed she could treat Anya. She reminded her who was really in charge and to never treat her as she had that morning. Her orders must always be obeyed or she'd report Anya's actions to her father—and she'd regret that. She glanced over at Ida—her prison guard. She would have to find a way to avoid her as much as possible. Somehow, she would find her way back home and out of Ana's body, but she wasn't sure how to go about accomplishing that.

"You are being a good girl," Ida said. "This is what you need to do. Your father has expectations for you." She patted her arm. "The trip to London was needed, but you belong here. Your wedding will be in a few months, and you need to accustom yourself to what your husband will wish from you."

She gagged. "Yes, Ida." Anya couldn't handle any of her platitudes anymore. "I'll make father proud." That seemed like something she should say, but it was the last thing she wanted to actually do. The more she learned about Edward Wegner, the more she hated him.

The car pulled into a long drive and came to a stop in front of a large building with high gates around it. They waited for the gates to open, and then they traveled inside. The car stopped again at the entrance. Time for her to face the things she wanted to avoid.

She stepped out of the car and paused for Ida. Once she was by Anya's side, they walked into the embassy together. In this one instance she was glad for Ida. The maid was a buffer of sorts. After they were inside, a servant welcomed them. "Miss Anastasia," the man greeted them. He was dressed in all black. His ebony hair was the nearly the same shade as his suit, and his silvery blue eyes were striking. They were an odd shade she found familiar. She couldn't look away, mesmerized by their beauty. "I've been assigned to be your guard. You're not to leave the embassy without me, your fiancé, or your father." She had no desire to leave in either her men's company. If she wanted to leave, she'd try to ensure it was in the company of her new guard.

She frowned. Great. Now she had another person that would be following her every move. She swallowed hard and nodded. "I understand... Mister..." Had he introduced himself? She couldn't recall in that moment.

"Arthur Jones," he said evenly in a no-nonsense tone. He kept his head held high and didn't move a muscle. "Ma'am."

He was a soldier. That made sense in a bodyguard. She didn't hold it against him. He was only doing his job, but that didn't mean she had to like it. "Mr. Jones," she said and smiled at him. "I have no intention of putting myself in danger. It's a perilous time in Germany, and I do not want to be a casualty to it. Thank you for doing your part to keep me safe."

He was quiet a moment before speaking. "Yes, ma'am." Had he expected her to put up a fuss? Anastasia was a proper lady in every sense of the word without actually having the title. Ana knew what was expected of her. Ida had ensured she understood her place on their trip to Germany. That was when Ida's strictness became evident and Anya learned quick to keep her thoughts to herself. "Now," she began. "If you'll excuse us." She gestured toward Ida. "It's been a long trip, and I'd like to rest." What she didn't say was she needed some time to herself. If she went to her chambers then Ida would leave her alone. She wouldn't feel as if her every move was being observed.

"Of course," he said and nodded. He moved aside so Anya and Ida could pass him. He wasn't handsome exactly, but definitely arresting. In another time, she might have taken an interest in him.

Ana wanted to glance back at him but kept her

focus in front of her. If she showed any interest in Arthur Jones, Ida would run and tattle on her. Besides, nothing could come of it. Anya didn't belong here, and Ana had a fiancé.

ANYA STARED out the window of her room. She'd been in Germany for a week now, and she'd made no progress in figuring out how to return home. She might have to resign herself to her current situation. Perhaps she should do something productive with her time in 1933. There was a great war coming and thousands would die. If she could, and was brave enough, it might be possible to save some of the people the Nazi government would target.

What if that was the reason she'd been sent here?

She sighed. If she hoped to make a difference, she'd have to leave her bedroom. Hiding wouldn't help anyone, especially herself. She could seek out Arthur Jones and have him accompany her out of the embassy since the only good thing about having a Nazi fiancé was it gave her a cover of sorts. No one should suspect her of helping Jews escape persecution. The problem was she had no idea how to go about finding and helping those in need. If she approached the wrong person it would get her killed or worse. There were worse things than dying…

With a sigh, she turned away from the window and went to the door and pulled it open. If she was going to start living, she had to take the first step. She walked down the hall and headed to Ana's father's office. Thinking of him in those terms kept it more formal and not real to her. She disliked the man intensely. He was far slimier in person than she had anticipated. Anya had yet to meet her fiancé, Dierk Eyrich. He was out of town doing an inspection on a concentration camp. They had not called it that, but Anya knew what it was. It was one of the worst camps to exist in history —Buchenwald. Not that any of the camps were good. They were all horrible, and so many had died.

She knocked on the door to Edward Wegner's office. After a few moments, he called out, "Come in."

Anya went inside and waited for him to address her. He sat behind a large mahogany desk, writing. After a few awkward moments of silence, he glanced up. "What can I do for you, Anastasia?"

"I'd like permission to attend the opera tonight." A lump formed in her throat, and she swallowed, trying to remove it, but it stubbornly stayed in place.

"The Berlin State Theater is having an encore performance of Richard Wagner's *Die Meistersinger von Nürnberg* tonight." She had overheard the ambassador's wife mention the opera performance. The ambassador and his wife had been sent an invitation, but they had declined it.

He didn't even glance at her as he began talking, "Dierk isn't here to escort you, and I don't wish to see the opera. I'm far too busy." He began to write frantically again. "This isn't important. Find something else to occupy your time with. When Dierk returns, he can help entertain you."

She had to convince him. Going to the opera was the first step she could take to further her goals. She had to ingratiate herself in German society. How else could she uncover plans regarding the capture of Jews? She didn't have any other means of gaining information. "I'd still like to attend. Can't Mr. Jones accompany me? He is my guard, isn't he? He'll see I'm kept safe and treated properly." Anya hoped Arthur wouldn't mind seeing some German propaganda. It would definitely be quite nauseating. She assumed he wasn't a Nazi sympathizer like Edward Wegner.

Edward glanced up and met her gaze. "You must

really wish to see this opera. What do you hope to gain from it?"

"Enlightenment," she said. It was the simplest answer and one this man would understand. He would think a female incapable of intelligent thought. After all, he'd traded his daughter to a Nazi for his own purposes.

"You hope to learn something?" He chuckled softly. "You?" Edward Wegner shook his head as if the very idea was ridiculous. "You're a simple girl. I doubt you'll gain much knowledge from the opera. It'll all go right over your pretty little head."

Anya gritted her teeth. He was beyond horrid. "I'd like to see for myself and listen to what the opera's message is." In that, she wasn't lying. Even though she knew it was Nazi propaganda, she wanted to listen to it. The idea behind it would only help her understand them more and learn how to help those that needed it.

"If it means that much to you," he began, "I'll arrange it with Mr. Jones." He set his pen down. "I expect you to only attend the performance. You'll leave a half hour before and return immediately after."

"Thank you, Father," she said and glanced to the

floor. He would expect a little bit of humility and cowardice from his daughter. If Anya looked at him directly in the eyes, Edward Wegner wouldn't react well. Ida's instructions had been exact. Her father expected her to act a specific way, and if she failed to do so, he'd punish her. Ida had taken great pleasure in explaining how those reprimands would go too. She had no reason not to believe the maid so she'd paid attention to everything Ida said. "I'll do as you directed."

"See that you do," he said firmly. "Now go. I have work to do, and you've disrupted me enough." He had no respect for his daughter. When he was done with her, he acted as if she was no longer in the room. Anya wished she could make it better for Ana somehow. Maybe it would be after she started helping the Jews in Germany.

Anya nodded and turned to leave the room—not that Edward Wegner noticed. She didn't have anything else to say to him anyway, and she had to ensure her plan went off without a hitch. It helped that her fiancé was gone...even if she was disgusted by what kept Dierk Eyrich occupied. She would use that to her advantage, along with his knowledge of the camp if she could manage it. She could act sweet and innocent to lure him into speaking about things he shouldn't. Anya wasn't an actress, but how hard could it be?

She went down the hall and headed back to her bedchamber. Now that she had permission, she had to prepare for the evening. Starting with her gown. After she knew what to wear, she would prepare a bath and have a good soak. It wouldn't be a fun evening, but that didn't mean she couldn't look and feel pretty.

CHAPTER FOUR

The bath had been wonderful. Anya felt renewed and ready for a night at the opera. She sat at the vanity and dressed her hair in what she hoped was a fashionable style for the time period. If she were in her own body, her hair wouldn't be nearly long enough for any elaborate styles. Her hair color was similar to Ana's, but that was where it ended. Ana had long, honey-blonde hair, and Anya's is more of a shoulder-length, burnished-blonde. She supposed the blonde hair worked well for Ana's father. With the Nazi belief of the Aryan race being superior, she definitely looked the part... Not that she found that fact particularly appealing, but with all things, she would use what she could to her advantage.

With her hair done, it was time to finish dressing. She'd been careful to pick a dress she wouldn't need Ida's help with; thankfully, most didn't require her maid's assistance. Anya despised the woman and wished she could dismiss her and find a new maid. She didn't know how Ana managed to deal with her every day. Perhaps Ana had realized it would be easier for her if she didn't need Ida to assist her and ordered them that way. Anya couldn't be certain. She wasn't well acquainted with 1930s fashion.

The dress she'd chosen to wear was a delicate, embroidered, blush pink mesh over a matching silk lining. It was elegant and ethereal with a sultry scoop neckline and buttoned down the side. The embroidered mesh split toward the bottom of the hemline, giving it a luxurious appearance. Anya loved it. Sometimes it felt good to dress up and go out. She hadn't done anything so extravagant in ages. Now that she didn't have much choice and was far from being herself, it felt silly that she'd worked so hard and forgot what it was like to play a little.

She finished her ensemble with a pair of pink and white two-tone T-strap heels. Anya sighed and took one more look at herself in the mirror. She still couldn't resign herself to looking at another person instead of herself. Maybe after she did a few good deeds she'd earn her way back home. She didn't belong in this era and she didn't want to experience the Holocaust first-hand. This was a nightmare she couldn't wake herself from.

Satisfied with what she saw in the mirror, she grabbed her white fur wrap and put it over her shoulders, tying it in place with the silk ribbon, then left the sanctity of her bedchamber. It was the only place she felt remotely safe, and even there, Ida intruded more than Anya liked. Arthur Jones would be waiting for her, and she hated being late. She hoped he was not irritated that he had to attend the opera with her.

The performance would be all in German, and she knew very little of the language. She could make out a word here or there, but she had never cared to truly learn it. She was both grateful and irritated she wouldn't be able to understand much. Grateful because the propaganda would be truly atrocious and irritated because it would make eavesdropping on conversations harder.

Perhaps Mr. Jones spoke some of the language… Would he be willing to eavesdrop for her? She would have to ask him a few discreet questions and see how he felt about the Germans and what they were doing to the Jews. She didn't know anyone in this time, and she didn't want to make a fatal mistake. Edward Wegner had chosen him as her guard. He must trust Mr. Jones for a reason. The last thing she needed was for him to tattle to the man who was supposed to be her father.

There were several sections and entrances to the embassy. She wasn't required to use the main one because she lived in residence. It made it easier to leave when she was allowed to step outside of the embassy. When she reached the foyer in the part of the embassy where she was housed, Mr. Jones was already there waiting on her. He was dressed in a dark suit, a crisp white shirt, and black tie. His ebony hair was brushed back, making his cobalt eyes even more vivid. He was devastating to behold. Her breath caught in her throat, and she had to remind herself to breathe. If she wasn't careful, she could quickly become enamored of this stoic gorgeous man.

"You look lovely," he said and held his arm out to her. "Are you ready for an entertaining evening."

She placed her arm over his and nodded. "Of course." Anya barely remembered to smile. "It's been a little stifling in the embassy. A bit of fresh air will be a welcome change."

"If you wished to go outdoors all you had to do

was ask." He led her to the door, and they exited the embassy. "I would be happy to accompany you wherever you wish to go."

She was glad he was willing because she fully intended to take him up on his offer. Though she would prefer to do it when her fiancé was not in Berlin. It would make her reasons for having Mr. Jones accompany her make more sense. Dierk wasn't supposed to return for another week. She would take advantage of his absence as much as possible.

"I don't know how much my father will allow." She nibbled on her bottom lip. "He's a bit overprotective." More like overbearing and controlling.

"He has good reason to be. It's quite tumultuous in Germany these days." He let go of her arm to open the car door for her. Mr. Jones gestured toward the seat, and Anya slipped into the car. He shut the door and then went over to the driver side. Once he was in the car, he started to speak again, "I'll keep you safe. I promise. If you want, I can give you a tour of the city and show you some of my favorite places."

"I would like that," she replied, her tone quiet. Did Mr. Jones have feelings for Ana or was it her, Anya, he liked? She was suddenly filled with so much self-doubt it made her ache. Ana didn't know what she should or should not do. What if she started something with him and messed up Ana's life or her own? What if she was stuck in this time in Ana's body? Shouldn't she try to explore all the possibilities?

"Make yourself comfortable." He smiled and then started the car. "We will be at the opera in no time."

Anya took that as a reason to remain silent. She was at a loss for words anyway. He had given her something else to contemplate, and she didn't know how to feel about any of it.

MR. JONES HAD BEEN CORRECT. It hadn't taken long to reach the opera, and she hadn't had nearly enough time to think. He parked the car, and they strolled toward the entrance. They had given the ambassador a box, and he'd given his staff permission to use it in his place. His wife had heard that Anya wanted to attend the opera performance and had written her a note to reiterate that authorization. Anya liked the ambassador and his wife. They were kind and intelligent people, and nothing like Edward Wegner. Why couldn't Anya have had a father similar to the ambassador? He would be much easier to deal with and was far kinder in the long term.

She sighed.

"What's wrong?" Mr. Jones asked. His tone was filled with concern, but his expression remained blank.

"Nothing," she said quickly. "It's a lovely evening isn't it?"

He nodded but didn't meet her gaze. His focus was on their surroundings. He looked everywhere but at her. That was his job, she supposed. Mr. Jones had to be aware of what happened around her, and as long as she didn't go wild, he could do his job assured of where she was. Anya didn't know much about what a bodyguard did, but she couldn't find fault in Mr. Jones. At least, not so far. "The weather is fair. Before long it will be bitter cold."

Anya wrinkled her nose. "I hate winter." She shivered. "Honestly, I hate being cold. The snow is pretty, but it's also messy and annoying. Wouldn't it be nice to live someplace that is warm all the time?"

"I actually do," he began. "I'm from California. We have nice weather most days."

She'd never traveled to the States, but she couldn't admit that. Ana was supposed to be American. Though, from the way her father treated her, she doubted Ana had traveled beyond New York.

"I've never been to California. It must be lovely there."

"It is," he said. "One of the greatest places on Earth. I look forward to returning."

He was being more open than he had been in their previous conversations. Not that there had been many, but he didn't seem to want to give her too many details about himself. Interestingly, he felt comfortable enough to do so now. "What made you decide you wanted to be a bodyguard."

He chuckled softly. "I joined the army when I turned eighteen. They taught me everything I know." He went quiet a moment. "This is all I know." His words were mumbled, but she'd heard them clearly. He didn't expand on his statement, but she wanted to know more. Didn't he want something more for his life? Did he have no real ambition? She'd have to remember to ask him all of that later.

They reached the entrance, and they gave their names to the doorman. They were given tickets and shown to the ambassador's box. Once they were seated, she scanned the room. There wasn't much to tell about the people there to see the performance. They were all dressed in finery, and almost all of them fit the ideal German citizen, according to Adolf Hitler. They were mostly blond, as well as a few people with hair that various shades of red. She couldn't help wondering if perhaps some might be Jews with dyed hair. They would do what they could to hide in plain sight. It sickened her they had to do all that to stay alive and be treated like humans should. The entire situation was just wrong in so many ways.

Anya turned to Mr. Jones. "Tell me something about yourself."

He lifted a brow, and his lips twitched a little. That hint of a smile gave her hope. He wanted to talk, and that was all that mattered to her. "Haven't I already done so?"

"Have you?" She tilted her head to the side. "I don't recall."

"I admitted where I'm from," he reminded her.

She waved her hand dismissively. "That's nothing. I want you to tell me something personal." Anya leaned a little closer. "Something I can't learn from anyone else but you."

He turned away from her and studied the crowd. Had she pushed him too far? She wanted to know more about him, and the only way to do that was to ask questions and urge him to open up to her. Maybe if she told him something about herself, he'd see it as a peace offering. But what could she say that would be safe? She wanted to be honest, be Anya, and still not give herself away as not being Ana. "I love poetry." He didn't acknowledge her. "My favorite poem is by Tennyson." She closed her eyes and quoted her favorite verse from "Maud."

> "'Half the night I waste in sighs,
> Half in dreams I sorrow after,
> The delight of early skies;
> In a wakeful doze I sorrow,
> For the hand, the lips, the eyes,
> For the meeting of the morrow,
> The delight of happy laughter,
> The delight of low replies.'"

He turned toward her and stared as if he had never seen her before. Had she blundered? Her stomach fluttered as she waited for him to say something. She hadn't realized how much she wanted him to like her until that moment.

"Tennyson?" He shook his head and then sighed. "I like poetry too. He's good, but I prefer Keats." Then he did something she never would have expected. He leaned over and whispered a line from one of Keats's love poems, "'Of love, your kiss,—those hands, those eyes divine.'"

She shivered as her body came alive. His husky tone made her warm all over, and she wanted to lean into him. She turned her head and met his gaze. There was heat there. He *was* attracted to her. There was no denying that anymore. They both felt something, and it should terrify her, but instead vibrate with need.

They were mesmerized with each other, and the spell didn't break until the lights went low and the curtains were raised. Even then, they didn't look away until the first notes of the opera filled the theater. Anya made herself glance away from him and at the stage. If she didn't, she would have kissed him, and that would not have gone well. They were in public, and she was supposed to be engaged. Edward Wegner would have her head if she ruined his daughter's reputation. She took a deep breath and made herself focus. Maybe, sometime later, when they were alone in a private place, she could explore what this had all meant. Now was not that time, but soon, she promised herself.

CHAPTER FIVE

A couple of days after the opera, Anya still could not shake Mr. Jones from her thoughts. She couldn't bring herself to think of him by his first name. It seemed too intimate somehow while trying not to fall for a man she couldn't have. When she found a way home, she would have to leave him behind, and she didn't want her heart to remain in the past forever. That would be a terrible fate.

She wandered to the library to search for a novel to read. Edward Wegner didn't allow her to do much. Even her choice of books was limited. If she found something that was outside of her allowed reading material, she'd have to find a way to sneak it to her room and hide it from Ida. So far, she had managed to read *Pride and Prejudice* without the maid discovering it. Edward thought anything romantic frivolous. It was a good thing he didn't have control of what books were shelved in the library. The ambassador had brought some of his personal books with him, and Ana took advantage of it. That was why she waited until most of the residents retired to their bedchambers for the night before searching the library in peace. That was what she did now.

Anya glanced down the hall and then quickly bolted to down the corridor. She stopped at the end and checked to make sure it was clear, and then quickly went to the library door, pulled it open, and slipped inside, shutting the door behind her as quick as possible. She leaned against it, placing her hand over her chest, taking a deep, relieved breath.

"What are you hiding from?" a man asked.

Anya jumped, startled by his voice. She banged her head against the door. "Ouch," she muttered as she lifted her hand to her head. "Did you have to scare me?"

"My apologies," Mr. Jones said contritely. "It was not my intention to frighten you."

She was grateful it was Mr. Jones and not, well, anyone else. He seemed to want to truly protect her and wouldn't purposely get her in trouble. Anya stood completely still to give her rapidly beating heart time to slow. She took a deep breath and studied him. This was the most relaxed she'd ever seen him. He sat on the leather sofa leaning against the arm of it. His black jacket had been laid across the arm, and his tie loosened around his neck.

"It's all right," she reassured him. "I was not expecting anyone to be in the library this late."

"Why are you here at this hour?" he lifted a brow. He leaned forward slightly, then pressed his elbows on to his knees and placed his chin onto his folded hands as he waited for her to respond.

She swallowed hard. Something about the look in his eyes made her nervous. What did he expect her to say? More importantly, what did he think he knew about her? Surely, he couldn't have realized she wasn't really Ana. She'd played the part as best she could, but she could have made a mistake. This wasn't the first time Ana had been to Berlin. She'd only been allowed to go to London to visit the Duke and Duchess because Edward Wegner believed it a good idea to cultivate the relationship. She had learned that on the trip back to Berlin. It was one of the things Ida had not stopped talking about.

She met Mr. Jones's gaze. "I was having trouble sleeping and decided to find something to read."

"You hoped to find a good book to make you sleepy?" He lifted his head and relaxed back into the couch. He gestured to the numerous shelves. "Don't let me stop you from searching."

Now that she knew he was in the library, she loathed the idea of leaving quickly. She wanted a reason to stay, but wasn't certain what would be believable. Perhaps she should start browsing and hope something would come to her as she looked over the books. "Don't mind if I do," she told him and marched across the room. The first shelf she came across had several books of poetry. Should she snag a book of Keats? She had read a couple of his poems in the past. It was why she'd recognized the one line of "To Fanny" that he'd spoken to her at the opera. She didn't recall the whole poem though. It might be good to read it over. Though she didn't really wish to do so in his company. That would have to wait for another time. She moved away from the poetry and onto the next shelf.

Anya ran her fingers over the spines and stopped at the section of Charles Dickens novels. She had read a few, but she had been hoping to read *Great Expectations*. Perhaps she should start with that.

Instead, an idea came to her. She turned toward Mr. Jones who hadn't moved from the couch. Had he been watching her the entire time? "Do you have a favorite novel?"

He shook his head. "I don't have time for frivolous entertainment."

"But you quoted Keats to me," she reminded him. "How is that not frivolous and reading a novel is?"

He chuckled lightly. "That is the remnants of a foolish boy who saw the romantic side of the world. I'm no longer that sentimental or naïve. I haven't been for a very long time." Mr. Jones came to his feet and walked toward her. He lifted his hand and brushed a stray lock behind her ear. She shivered at his touch. "Sometimes I wish I was, but there is no returning to what we once were."

She tilted her head to the side. "I hope you're wrong."

"I'm not," he said firmly. There was a harshness in that tone that was immovable. Nothing she said would convince him he was wrong.

She moved out of his reach and turned back to the shelf and snagged the copy of *Great Expectations*. Anya didn't want to be in the library any longer. It hurt too much to feel something for him and know she couldn't do anything about it. This wasn't her life to mess with. She had to believe at some point she'd return to where she belonged, and it would be horrible for Ana to return it and find herself in an untenable situation. She turned back to him. "You do not know what you're missing. Sometimes it is nice to escape from reality for a little while. Especially when life is particularly terrible."

"Is your life that unpleasant then?" He'd stepped closer to her, and if he moved one step more, there would be no more space between them.

"What if it was? Would you save me?" She couldn't tell him there was nothing he could do to help her. How could he? Anya didn't even know how to save herself. She doubted anyone would.

"I could try," he said softly. "This place, the danger it presents, you don't belong here." She started at his statement. He was right. She didn't belong in this time, but she couldn't tell him that. Regardless, he wasn't speaking of time travel, but of Germany and the war on the horizon.

"Perhaps," she agreed. "But my fate is sealed." The more she thought about it, the more she believed she was stuck in 1933. She didn't know why, but she had come to this time for a reason. "There is nothing you can save me from."

He closed his eyes and took a deep breath as if

fighting for control. "Are you certain? Let me prove you wrong."

"How?" her voice was barely above a whisper. She slid her tongue across her lips quickly.

"Let me give you that tour of Berlin. I'd like to show you something." She didn't know what she'd expected, but an invitation to tour Germany hadn't been even close.

What would it hurt? She nodded. "All right. Tomorrow we will go. Providing my...father." She nearly stumbled over calling Edward Wegner that. "Approves of the outing."

"I'll see that he does." He leaned down and pressed his lips to hers in a quick kiss, then turned on his heels and left. Anya lifted her fingers to her lips. They still tingled from his kiss. She hadn't realized until he'd done it, but she'd been hoping he'd kiss her. Now she couldn't wait for their day together... What was he going to show her? How would it prove anything?

She cradled the book in her arms and left the library, careful to ensure no one saw her. Anya had come this far without being caught, and it would not help for someone to discover her nightly visits to the library now. Once she was in her room, she hid the book and crawled into bed. She had no desire to read any longer, and had too much to ponder over to focus. Instead, she tossed and turned all night, sleep impossible because of that chaste kiss.

ANYA DRESSED THE NEXT MORNING, not as bright-eyed and alert as she would have liked. She would not miss what she had planned with Mr. Jones this day though. Whatever he had to show her…she desperately wanted to see. So, she'd work through her exhaustion. Perhaps later she could nap or even retire early. As long as she was inside the embassy, no one paid that close attention to her. She was a good girl, after all. Anya rolled her eyes. No one truly knew her if they believed that. Not that any of them would considering they had no idea who she really was or that Ana was no longer accounted for.

She left her room and headed to the foyer. When she had awakened, she had found a note on her bedside table. She didn't want to discover how Arthur Jones had managed to sneak it into her bedroom without her realizing it. She must have slept at least a little for that to happen. He had left instructions on what time and where to meet him. By sheer luck, she'd managed to wake up in time to follow what he'd wrote. Otherwise, he'd have been left to do his little tour on his own.

Mr. Jones was leaning against the wall with his arms crossed. When he noticed her, he stood up straight and his lips tilted upward and happiness exuded from him. His smile was devastating. He'd always looked so stern before. This was the first time she'd ever beheld him in any other fashion, and a smile on Arthur Jones was something she hoped to see more often in the future.

"Are you ready?" he asked.

"As much as I will ever be," she said. Her voice was still hoarse, and she hadn't had time to eat breakfast. All she'd had was a bit of water after she'd brushed her teeth.

"Come along then," he said, and they exited the embassy. "We will drive for a bit, and then the rest of the day we will be walking."

"This tour will take all day?" She hadn't counted on that. "What are you going to show me?"

"That is the plan," he told her. "It will be fun. I promise."

They headed to the car, and he held the door open for her. She slid inside and waited for him to join her. He sat in the driver's seat and started the engine, then shifted the gearshift and headed to the gate of the embassy, and when they opened, he drove away from the embassy and toward a part of Berlin that Anya had never visited. Anya hoped she wouldn't come to regret this decision. He drove along the river until he reached a bridge to take him to an island. Once he reached a point he could no longer drive, he parked the car.

"Here we are," he said. "One of the best parts of the city. This is Museum Island."

They started down the first path. Mr. Jones shoved his hands into his pockets. Did he do that so he could resist temptation? She wanted to move closer to him, but held back. If they were seen in public acting in anything resembling an intimate fashion, it would come back to haunt her, and perhaps him as well.

When they reached the first building in their path, he pointed to it. "That is the Neues." He was quiet a moment and then continued, "It houses the Egyptian exhibits and the prehistoric as well. There are some fascinating early historical collections, and one of the artifacts is a bust of the Egyptian queen Nefertiti."

"But we are not going in there to see it?" She would very much like to browse the Egyptian artifacts. Mummies had always fascinated her. It was perhaps a little perverse, but she would like to study them if at all possible. Maybe sometime later, if she returned to her time.

"If we have time... There is a museum I'd much rather take you inside of, and I believe will interest you more than the earliest historical time periods."

"Really?" She lifted a brow. "What does it house?"

"Some wonderful works of art," he began. His tone held a mischievous tone. "Come. I'll show you."

They went inside the museum. He remained silent as they walked through some of the galleries. When they reached one section, he stopped and pointed to a painting. "This is *Telemachus' Return* by Eberhard von Wächter."

The painting depicted a group of ladies as they watched over a soldier, Greek if she had to make a guess, that was hugging another woman, possibly his wife. They appeared to care a great deal about each other.

"You like this painting?" She turned to him. "What is it that draws you to it?"

There was something almost ethereal about it. She couldn't help wondering about their story. Where had he been and how long had he been gone? Was their love eternal? Did they have regrets? It was both comforting and disconcerting at the same time. Anya had never loved anyone that much.

"I like to think, one day, I'll have something like this." He motioned toward the painting. "Someone to love, a home, a family. This type of emotion, the sense of purpose, it isn't so easy to find. Once my duty is finished here in Germany, I'm going to return home. I hate this country and its newfound ideals. It is hard to stomach." He met her gaze. "But there is beauty here too. This art is proof of that. Nothing is all bad or all good, but pure evil is not difficult to see."

What was he trying to say to her? "Have you seen so much evil then?"

"More than I would like," he admitted. "I wanted you to see some of the good in Berlin. One day it might be difficult to find. For now, though, there is this." He pointed to the painting. "Any time you need to get away and feel as if there is something in this world worth observing. Let me know, and I'll take you."

What he didn't say in that statement was: *I'll do anything for you, to protect you. Say the word, and I will see you through any storm.* It was breathtaking, and she lost all ability to speak. The rest of the day, through everything they viewed, she didn't say much. He had given her a lot to think about, and perhaps, later, she'd tell him her truth. That she wasn't Ana, but Anya from nearly two decades in the future. Hopefully, when she did tell him the truth, he wouldn't think her insane and tell everyone she should be put in a mental asylum. She swallowed a lump that formed in her throat. She had to find the right opportunity to tell him and take a leap of faith.

CHAPTER SIX

One week later...

*A*nya stared out the window of the library, wishing she could go outside on her own. She didn't want to bother Mr. Jones again. He'd been nothing but kind to her, and she felt horrible taking advantage of his generosity. Surely he had other duties at the embassy besides guarding her. She didn't dare pick another book, at least not in the middle of the day. Anyone could walk in and catch her doing something her father deemed imprudent for a woman.

"Ah, there you are," a man with a thick German accent said in perfect English. Anya turned, afraid it was Ana's long absent fiancé.

Slowly she glanced away from the window and looked in the direction of where the sound of the man's voice had originated. He had blond hair cropped short on the side, but remained thick and wavy on top. His blue eyes were piercing and almost harsh in appearance—there didn't seem to be one inkling of kindness in their depths. Her stomach churned at the very idea of spending any time in this man's company. Poor Ana... Anya hated that, when she finally found a way to return home, the real Ana would be stuck living with this man. She had little doubt that he was indeed Dierk Erich. "Hello," she greeted him, ensuring she kept her voice low and her demeanor as demure as possible.

"What have you been doing while I've been away?" He crossed the room and pressed his thumb to her chin to lift her head up to meet his gaze. "Have you done something you shouldn't have?"

Plenty...but she wasn't about to admit that to Dierk. He didn't seem like the type to take that sort of admission well. For all she knew, he might beat her. "No," she said, then swallowed hard. "I went to the opera and visited Museum Island, but nothing else."

He lifted a brow. "Did your father escort you?"

His tone suggested he didn't like her answer. It was too late to take her response back.

"He sent a guard with me." Hopefully he accepted that. Her heart beat rapidly inside her chest as she waited for him to respond. She hated this. Why did she have to wake up where she didn't belong? Anya wanted to go home...to the life she knew. This constant uncertainty was playing havoc on her emotional state.

"I suppose that is acceptable." He pulled her into his arms and pressed his lips against her forehead. It took everything inside of her not to pull away from him. Her skin crawled at his touch. She couldn't help wishing it was Mr. Jones who held her instead of Dierk.

"Did your trip go well?" She wanted him to leave. What would it take for him to go? It was horrid, but she almost wished he had gone anywhere else. He was a bad man, and anywhere he went he'd cause havoc. Anya hated how selfish it made her to want him gone. Someone should ensure he experienced the same pain he inflicted on others. Though she doubted it would make him even remotely empathetic. She didn't like him, and she'd only met him a few moments ago.

"It was a bit of unpleasantness," he answered,

then stepped away from her. He walked over to a nearby table that had several decanters of alcohol displayed. She'd never been tempted to have any of it. Anya hated alcohol, though sometimes she liked a nice glass of wine. Yet if she had decided to pour a glass, several of the embassy's inhabitants would have given her some odd looks. Dierk poured some scotch into one of the crystal glasses next to the decanters. "I don't want to worry you over the trivial details." He lifted the glass to his lips and took a sip. "I'd rather discuss our upcoming wedding."

She'd rather walk over broken glass. "Of course," she said, at a loss. Anya couldn't very well admit she had no idea when the wedding was supposed to take place. "What do you have on your mind?"

"We should set a date now that you're back in Germany," he said, then took another drink of his Scotch. "We've delayed it long enough."

Anya would delay it forever if she could. "If that is what you wish to do. What date did you have in mind?" She could barely get the question out. What if she had to go through with the ceremony and become his wife? She could barely stand his touch, and to share a bed with him? Anya couldn't do it. She wouldn't. For now, she'd go through the motions and pretend that the wedding would go as planned. If, when the time came where she had to put on a pretty dress and say vows to this man, she'd bolt. She'd be the runaway bride that made it a fashion trend. No one deserved to be married to a man they didn't love, let alone one that could be potentially abusive.

"I'd prefer it be soon." He finished the drink and set the empty glass on the table. "A week if it can be arranged."

Panic seized her, and she forgot how to breathe. A week? Had he lost his mind? A wedding couldn't be arranged that fast. At least not an elaborate one… It also wouldn't give her much time to make a desperately needed escape. "I don't know if my father would like that. He wanted something that he could invite everyone to. Wouldn't we need to give people time to commit attending? Then there is the…" She wasn't certain she was using the right terminology. *Drat.* "Ball afterward."

"Do you think that is necessary? We can have an intimate ceremony and a small dinner afterward."

She held back the urge to gag. "That is possible. I can speak to him, but even something small would need more than a week." She hoped for a month, but would settle for a fortnight.

"I will discuss it with your father, and when we settle on a date, I'll inform you."

How kind of him. She wouldn't roll her eyes, she wouldn't. "Wonderful." Anya gritted her teeth. There was only so much she could refrain from doing. "May I be excused? I'm feeling a little fatigued."

"You do look pale," he told her. "Very well." He brushed a stray lock behind her ear. "Go rest. You'll need to look your best for the grand ball later tonight."

She nearly choked. "The ball?" Why had no one informed her she was required to go out? What good was it to have a maid that watched her every move if she didn't update her on her required events.

"Yes," he confirmed, his tone held a hint of annoyance. "The ball. Wear your best gown. The Führer himself is expected to attend."

If she didn't want to go before, that news made her want to run, not walk, to the nearest train and leave Germany forever. "I am looking forward to meeting him." Too bad she couldn't poison him and prevent what the world was about to suffer. "Until later," she said and then turned on her heels to leave the library. Anya couldn't get away from him fast enough.

ANYA STOOD in her bedchamber as her maid buttoned up the back of her gown. She wished, not for the first time in the past couple of hours, she could skip the blasted ball. Dierk would not let her. Not that she'd asked to be excused… The little she knew of him had told her everything. He was very much like Ana's father. Too controlling and completely condescending toward women. He would view Anya as his property. Hell, he already did…

"Are you done yet?" Anya asked. She wanted this evening over with.

Ida reached out and smacked Anya's cheek. "Don't get sassy with me."

"Ouch," Anya muttered and rubbed her cheek. "That hurt."

"Maybe next time you'll keep your impertinence in check." Ida yanked on the dress. "There. Now sit so I can dress your hair."

Anya would have liked to slap Ida back, but held back the urge. The maid would likely hurt her worse for fighting back. Sometimes it was easier to accept the circumstances you were in than to continue struggling against them. So she sat and let Ida yank her hair into a tight chignon that made her head hurt.

"It's lovely," she told Ida, and it was. Sometimes fashion could be painful, and this particular hairstyle definitely fit that description. "May I please leave my room now?"

"Yes," she said. "Your fiancé will be waiting for you. Go now and do not dawdle and keep him waiting."

Someday, she hoped, Ida would find someone else to harass. Someone who might appreciate her heavy handedness. That someone was definitely not her. "Thank you, Ida." She understood her part even if she didn't want to play it.

She left the room and headed toward the foyer. Dierk was there waiting for her. He'd dressed in a dark blue suit that matched his eyes. His blond hair was slicked back, making him appear even creepier than he had earlier that day. Edward Wegner was in a deep conversation with him and hadn't even noticed her arrival. Mr. Jones stood off to the side in his black suit with too observant gaze. She smiled softly, but he didn't return it. Why did she feel guilty? She'd done nothing wrong...

Dierk finally noticed her. "I see you're finally ready," he said, annoyance in his voice. He looked her up and down and then nodded. "You're presentable. We must go now."

Edward Wegner frowned. "Don't you have a better dress than that?"

"No father," she said primly. "Ida said this is my best gown."

"You'll need something nicer for the wedding. I'll have a designer come to the embassy and prepare something special."

She nearly groaned. "The wedding will be even more wonderful with a new dress." Had he intended her to wear something she already owned? She was glad this wasn't her actual wedding. If she ever married, she wanted it to be special. Not some thrown together affair that was best forgotten. "Thank you."

"Come," Edward said to her, then nodded at Mr. Jones, gesturing that they needed to leave. There was something different about Mr. Jones...his eyes seemed darker, and he didn't seem to even notice her. He usually nodded toward her or flashed her a grim smile of some sort. She'd ponder over it later... "We don't want to be late."

Considering she didn't want to go at all, she as all right with that. Neither Dierk nor Edward would want to hear that though. "I'm ready," she said and waited for them to indicate she could exit.

Dierk went out the door first, then Edward, and Mr. Jones gestured for her to go after them. Apparently, the idea of ladies first had not occurred to her fiancé or father. She couldn't help thinking again... poor Anastasia. Mr. Jones followed behind her and helped her into the car, then got into the driver seat. She hadn't expected he would drive them, but she should have. Why else had he been waiting?

It didn't take them long to reach the grand assembly hall. Swastika flags were hanging down the building and armed guards were standing outside. This all seemed like she was living in a different reality. Anya kept hoping she'd open her eyes and find out this was all a bad dream.

Mr. Jones pulled the car up to the entrance. A man opened the door and helped her out of. Dierk got out after her, and Edward stepped out from the front seat. Mr. Jones kept to himself and stayed in the car. Once everyone safely exited the car, he pulled away. She couldn't help glancing in his direction. Had she done something to anger him?

"Come along, dear," Dierk said as he grabbed her arm and looped it with his. "It's time to meet everyone."

At least this ball gave her the perfect opportunity to instill herself in German society. She might be able to learn something useful and help some of the Jews escape persecution. She pasted a smile on her face and prepared to pretend to enjoy herself.

CHAPTER SEVEN

A German ball was like any other ball. Champagne glasses were filled as fast as they were emptied. Most of the guests were inebriated or well on their way to becoming so. Anya had been sipping on the same glass of bubbly since she arrived. She didn't want to lose her wits and give anyone a reason to believe she wasn't Anastasia Wegner. So far, she hadn't slipped, but there was a first time for everything. Drinking and Anya didn't mix well, and she didn't want to take any unnecessary risks.

She didn't speak German, so that made some of the conversations difficult. Eavesdropping even more so... At least some of the guests spoke English and chose to humor her. Most of them ignored her though. No matter, she didn't want to talk to any of them. Her stomach had been one never-ending ball of unease since she'd woken up in the wrong time and the wrong body, but this…was so much worse than she could have imagined.

Dierk circled the room, talking to what seemed like everyone in attendance. She dutifully followed him from group to group and remained silent the entire time. She didn't ask any questions and kept her answers to as few words as possible. Dierk seemed to appreciate her demureness. Inside, she seethed. "This is my fiancée, Anastasia," he introduced her to another man. "We're to be married posthaste."

"Is that so?" the gentleman said with a bit of enthusiasm. "You're a lucky man. She is a beauty." As if that was the only attribute a woman had to offer. "And quiet too. Shows she knows her place."

Were all the men in this time misogynist gits? Should she speak or hold her tongue? She wasn't sure what was expected of her, and it scared her too much. None of this made any sense. Why was she lost in the past, and how could she ever find her way home?

"That she does," Dierk agreed. "The perfect wife. I couldn't ask for a better woman to have as my own." He slid his arm around her shoulders and pulled her close. Anya wrapped her arms around her middle in an attempt to still the rumbling in her stomach.

"I try," she mumbled. When could they go home?

"You do more than that." He practically beamed with pride. As if having a biddable wife was the greatest gift he could have been given. He was disgusting.

"At least you do not need to worry she'll give you inferior children. Not with her beautiful blonde hair and striking blue eyes," the man said. It occurred to her that Dierk had told him her name but hadn't done the same in kind. She had no idea what to call him. She supposed she could refer to him as *arse*, at least in her own thoughts. It fit all of the men she met at the damned ball. She was nothing but a mute broodmare to them.

"Did you hear about the Allendorfs?" the arse asked.

"No," Dierk replied. "What about them?" This was the first conversation they held entirely in English. That was odd. What purpose did they have for making her privy to any of what they had to say? The first part, about her, she supposed they thought was important for her to hear. Like it was praising her worthiness or something. This, though, sounded off, and they hadn't really said anything other than a name.

"They're harboring rats." Anger reverberated through his voice and his cheeks were tinged with red. "We're going to raid their home tomorrow morning before daybreak."

Her heart raced inside of her chest. Those poor people. She had no idea who the Allendorfs were, but she wished she could help them—find some way to warn them. Unfortunately, she didn't know anyone in German society. Even those she'd met tonight she'd never consider allies. She had never felt so helpless in her entire life.

"What a travesty. They had such potential to be one of the best German families." Dierk sighed. "Ah, well, there's nothing to do about it. An example must be made of them. No one goes against our cause without due punishment."

Anya swallowed hard. Was that warning meant for her? A reminder of who Anastasia was engaged to marry and what Dierk expected of her? He didn't know Anastasia was no more and that Anya had taken her place. Had she done something in the past that had given Dierk pause, or was Anya the one who had made him worry over what she might do?

She couldn't be certain either way, and she'd have to tread cautiously. If she hoped to help anyone, she had to be careful. It wouldn't do any good for her, or anyone, to get caught in the process.

"You are correct," the arse said. She really should find out the man's name. "Would you like to join us?"

"I enjoy a righteous raid," Dierk replied, then shook his head. "But I must leave the glory to you. My fiancée needs my attention, and I must see her home. I'll accompany you on your next assignment."

She would like to tell them there was no need for Dierk to see her home, but neither one would listen to her. Anya might as well hold her breath for all the good it would do her. Though this could be the opportunity to escape she'd been hoping for all night. "I am feeling fatigued," she said in a quiet voice. Hopefully he didn't question her and think she might be giving him any falsehoods—even though she was lying through her teeth. She couldn't stand him and would say almost anything to separate herself from him.

Dierk turned to meet her gaze. "You poor dear. It has been a long evening. I suppose we should say our goodbyes."

Anya would have rolled her eyes if she didn't fear he'd make her pay for the impertinence. "All right," she agreed, and kept her gaze lowered. Perhaps she was a better actress than she'd given herself credit for.

"Enjoy the rest of your evening, Oberst Bauer, and good luck dealing with one of our rat problems." *So that was his name...* Strange he had said his full name. Anya wondered why, but didn't question it too closely. She'd have to be careful not to raise his suspicion. "I trust you'll have them scurrying out of their hiding places without any difficulty."

"You may count on it," Oberst Bauer replied. "I'll have a report for you immediately following our raid."

"Good night," Dierk said, then turned to Anya. "Come, dear. Let's have our driver retrieve the car, and I'll take you home."

She let him lead her out of the ballroom and to the car. Partly because she didn't have a choice, and partly because there was nothing she wanted more than to leave. Anya couldn't wait to return to the embassy. Maybe once there she could figure out who the Allendorfs were, and then she might be able to save the Jews in their charge. What she didn't know was what she'd do with them once she found them. She had no place to hide anyone, and she didn't have anyone she could trust to aid her.

ALMOST EVERYONE WAS asleep at the embassy. After Dierk left, she'd went through the motions of preparing to sleep for the night. She wore her long chaste night-rail and slipped into bed. Sleep eluded her. Which was all right with her because she had plans. Ones that Ida did not need to be privy to…

She crawled out of bed once she deemed it safe, then dressed in a pair of dark trousers with a matching sweater. Anya wore a silk shirt underneath so it didn't chafe her breasts. She slipped on a pair of leather boots and tied the laces. With her clothes acceptable, she wound her long hair into a braid and then made it into a bun at the nape of her neck, then pulled a dark cap over her head. She wished she had some gloves…

Dierk had talked with Edward on the way home about the Allendorfs. Apparently, they were a wealthy family that lived on the opposite side of Berlin. The Jews they harbored were children. It sickened her to think they were raiding that house to take children to concentration camps, and then they'd punish the entire Allendorf family for sympathizing with their plight. The horridness of it was almost more than she could bear.

It had been too easy for her to uncover the information. She should be scared, but refused to give in to fear. Children depended on her to be brave. She barely had a plan in place. Most of it had been dressing in the clothing she'd secreted away days ago for an emergency. The next step of her plan was to steal one of the cars and drive to the Allendorf house. After that…she'd improvise where necessary.

She sneaked out of her bedchamber and moved as quietly as possible down the hallway. No one saw her, and she thanked whatever being helped aid her. That same being was most likely responsible for her current situation altogether, but she wasn't going to complain. She had to make it out of the embassy safely.

Anya stepped outside and rushed over to the garage and opened the door. She went inside and looked at the cars available. There were several cars to choose from. Did they really need this many available at the embassy? She stared at them for a moment and then went over to the closest one to the garage door.

She'd have to open that first… Anya had never had to open a garage door before. How did they work? She stared at it for several minutes, trying to figure it out, and frowned. This was going all wrong.

"Why are you in here?" a man asked.

Anya jumped, startled by the sound. She lifted her hand to her chest and took several breaths, then glanced up to meet Arthur Jones's gaze. "You scared me."

"I seem to be doing that a lot lately." He frowned. "You didn't answer my question." He didn't waver once as he stared at her. Anya didn't doubt for one second he would let her go without an explanation. Should she trust him? He didn't seem to like Dierk or even Edward Wegner, but that didn't mean he'd help her.

"I want to take one of the cars." Would he accept that and let her go without any more details? It might be too much to hope for, but what else did she have?

"Where are you going?" He folded his arms over his chest. "And why are you dressed this way?"

That would be much harder to explain. He wouldn't take a simple account of her plans. Anastasia probably never did anything she wasn't supposed to; Anya never followed the rules. She'd done so more than she wanted to since she'd woken up in the wrong time. She sighed. "Would you believe me if I said I wanted to remain anonymous?"

'Yes," he said. "The question is why."

He definitely wasn't going to make any of this easy for her. "I need to help some children." He might believe that. Especially since it was the truth. Surely he wouldn't stand in her way now that she'd been honest with him. He seemed like a good man.

"You're not in a position to help anyone," he reminded her. His voice was a combination of sternness and trepidation. "Are you trying to get yourself killed or worse?"

She stared at him. What was worse than being killed? She shook that thought away. Somehow, she didn't think she wanted to know the answer to that question. "No," she said quietly. "But I can't let them be hurt when I could have done something to prevent it."

He rubbed his hands over his face and let out a groan, then swore a few times. Arthur Jones paced several times and then stopped in front of her suddenly. "All right."

"All right?" She tilted her head to the side. "I don't understand."

"Has anyone ever told you that you're beautiful when you're confused?" Arthur asked.

"No," she replied, a little surprised at his statement. Then nibbled on her bottom lip. Not that it mattered much. He seemed to like Ana and but he had no idea what she truly looked like—he believed her to be someone else, and that troubled her. It shouldn't bother her, but it did. "That doesn't tell me anything either."

"All right, I'll help you." He gestured toward the car. "Get in. It's going to be a long night, and we don't have much time left."

Anya didn't stop to question his motivations. She was grateful for the help. It also surprised her a little he didn't question what she wanted to do. Though it shouldn't have... He'd been in the car too when Dierk and Edward had discussed the raid. Hopefully they wouldn't come to regret their decision to help those kids. They still had to make it to them in time.

CHAPTER EIGHT

*T*he moon was a mere sliver in the sky, ensuring that they would be shrouded in darkness. Mr. Jones parked the car at the end of the road behind some trees. He was much better at stealth than she could ever attempt to be. She should be thankful for his assistance; however, she still didn't understand why he'd agreed to help. What was his angle? Did he hope to gain something from her? If so, what? She hoped she hadn't made a grave error in judgment. He seemed like a good man, but sometimes appearances could be deceiving.

They walked through the trees, using them to cover their movements. Mr. Jones held up his arm, his hand in a fist. Anya stopped and waited for him to explain. "Someone is out there," he said in a low tone.

"What do we do?" she asked. Her hand shook a little and her stomach had turned into a knot of anxiety. She hadn't thought this through, clearly. What if they were discovered? What explanation could they possibly have for lurking in the woods outside of the Allendorf estate?

"We wait until they pass," he answered. "Then we move forward. I don't believe they're here for the kids. They may have been hired by the Allendorfs to patrol their grounds. Don't move until I tell you."

Anya remained completely still. She didn't want to die, and if she could help the children and continue to breathe after the night was over, she'd do whatever he deemed necessary to achieve that goal. Several moments passed by that felt as if they were hours. Later, if asked, she'd probably say she lost years off her life. It certainly aged her significantly in a short time. This was nothing like she'd ever experienced, or would. Anya wasn't nearly as brave as she'd thought. She wanted nothing more than to turn around and run back to the embassy. Deep inside she knew she had to go through with it though. If she gave in to her cowardice, she'd never forgive herself.

Mr. Jones held up his hand and waved it, motioning her forward. "They're gone. We don't have a lot of time." He turned his head and met her gaze in the darkness. She wished she could make out his expression, but the lack of light made it impossible. "Stay close."

She nodded, unable to speak. Her throat had gone dry and a lump had taken permanent residence there. Anya tried to swallow, but it wouldn't dislodge itself. No matter. She didn't need to use her voice anyway. Mr. Jones had taken charge, and she'd gladly follow his lead.

They began moving again. When they reached the edge of the woods, he stopped again and held up his arm in the same fashion. That must have been a signal he'd learned and expected her to understand. She hadn't. His stillness made her stop, not the gesture he gave her. Anya understood now though. She'd pay close attention to his actions and file them away for the future if she should need them. Not that she planned on doing anything like this again, but one could never be too prepared for what might happen.

"We will go to the back entrance," he told her. "They will come to the front first. We have a better chance of escape this way."

"All right," she agreed. It made sense, and he seemed to have more experience. It would be better to heed his advice. "Lead the way."

He didn't say anything to her. Instead, he turned away and started toward the rear of the house. Anya followed close behind. She was glad she'd decided to wear trousers. Doing this in a dress would have been awful. They reached the back, and he stopped again. "Stay here." They were by an outbuilding used for storage. "Do not come out unless you hear me say it is all right to do so."

"But…"

"Do not argue with me on this. I've humored you through this entire ordeal. I'll not put you in any more danger if I can help it." He stood completely still and waited. "Tell me you agree, or we will go back to the embassy now."

"Fine," she said through gritted teeth. "I'll wait, but I don't like it."

"You don't have to." He leaned down and pressed his lips to her forehead. Her heart fluttered from the affectionate gesture. She liked that he seemed to like her, might even love her; however, she couldn't ignore the fact he didn't really know her. He thought she was Anastasia Wegner. Even if she wanted to stay in this time, she couldn't have an honest relationship with him—could she? She didn't believe it, so she wouldn't allow herself to feel anything more than friendship for him. "As long as you are alive, that is all that matters right now."

If she told him the truth, it might ruin everything. He might never look at her the same whether he believed her or not. That kind of truth isn't something so easy to accept. She had thought she could tell him the truth, to take a risk, but the more she considered it the more she realized it would be a mistake. It was better she didn't say anything at all. Sometimes saying nothing was best, and sometimes the truth wasn't worth telling. There was no relationship to be had with Arthur.

With those words, he turned on his heels and headed to the house. She peeked around the outbuilding and kept her focus on his movements. Her heart thudded heavily, and the beats echoed through her ears. He'd be all right. There was no reason to worry. At least she prayed it would all turn out as it should.

He reached the door, lifted his hand, and knocked on it she assumed. No one came to answer it, so he repeated the action. After several seconds, the door opened. A small woman with short hair stood on the other side. Mr. Jones waved his hands and Anya presumed he was telling her what the issue was. The older woman lifted her hand to her chest and her mouth fell open, then she shooed him inside with a wave of her hand. The door quickly closed behind them.

Anya was alone in the darkness. All she could do was stay behind the outbuilding and hope it all went well. She wouldn't be able to live with herself if anything happened to Mr. Jones, the children, or the Allendorfs. She sank to the ground and leaned her head against the building.

She was a mess, and she had created one with her actions. Anya closed her eyes and reminded herself to breathe. A breath in, one out, and after several times repeating that action, she calmed. Mr. Jones would succeed. She refused to believe anything else.

ANYA DIDN'T KNOW how much more waiting she could take. It seemed as if she had been sitting alone for days. The sky had started to lighten a little, and that was not a good sign. Where were they? Edward Wegner had been surprisingly informed about the situation. That was how they had learned about the children. Two to be exact: a boy and a girl, both under ten years old. Edward had stated the girl was seven and the boy was eight, siblings parted from their parents who were already in concentration camps. Separated of course. The camps were not nice places that kept morale up by keeping families together.

She peeked around the side and stared at the door, willing it to open. Why had they not come out yet? Should she go knock on the door? Would Mr. Jones be angry with her if she did? He'd told her to remain there until he returned…but what if he never did? What should she do then? She could go back to the car and return to the embassy, but it might already be too late to do that. Ida would be rising soon and then would come to her bedchamber to wake her for the day. Once she realized Anya was gone, she'd raise the alarm. Anya had no choice. She had to wait and see this through, no matter the eventual outcome.

The door cracked open, and the old woman stood there. She glanced around the back yard then widened the space to step outside. She turned toward the entrance and motioned for someone to come out. Mr. Jones stepped out with the two children, both dark-haired and scrawny and had nothing but the clothes on their backs. How could anyone believe those two waifs were dangerous? They didn't mean anyone harm. None of the Jews had. She'd change the entire Holocaust if she could. The tragedies that would follow Hitler's reign would be remembered forever. No one would forget what he'd done in the name of his crusade to rid the world of the Jewish population. The genocide that would be known around the world for years and years...

Mr. Jones led the children over to the outbuilding. When they reached her, he held out his hand to help her to her feet. "We need to run. They'll be here to search the house soon."

He didn't have to tell her twice. She rushed behind him and the children; they went into the woods. The fast pace they kept made it difficult to avoid tree branches. Several swung back and hit her face, leaving stinging pain in their wake. She ignored them and kept moving. She could endure some minor pain if it meant these children would remain safe.

When they reached the car, her heart beat in a rapid staccato. She might not survive after all if she couldn't calm down. Mr. Jones went to the trunk and opened it. "I know it won't be comfortable," he told the children. "Remember what we discussed?"

"Stay under the blanket and remain silent," the

boy said. "We understand." The little girl trembled, and her brother wound his arm around her to comfort her. "Don't worry, Johanna. I'll keep you safe."

"I know you'll try, Oskar," she said softly. Her lips shaking as she spoke. "But even you can't promise that."

They were so old for being so young. She didn't have the worries they had when she was a child. Anya hadn't been forced to grow up well before she should have. The Nazi's were monsters for doing this to so many people. No one should feel persecuted. "We will do our best to protect you," she promised.

"That's all you can do," Oskar said solemnly. "We thank you for helping us."

"You're welcome," she said. "Now follow Mr. Jones' instructions. We've dallied long enough."

The children climbed into the storage space in the car and slid underneath a blanket. The lump returned to her throat. Now that they had the children, what would they do with them? She hadn't planned this far ahead. She didn't know if Mr. Jones had either. What should she do? Mr. Jones closed the hatch and turned to her. "Are you ready?"

"Mr. Jones…?"

"Don't you think it's time you called me Arthur?" He lifted a brow. "We are committing what many Germans believe is a crime together. We should be more familiar with each other."

He made a valid argument. Still, she remained reluctant to use his given name. What was she? A woman from the twentieth century, or did she belong in Regency where there were even stricter social norms? "All right, Arthur, then you should call me Anya." *Drat.* She'd slipped and said her real name.

"Anya?" He frowned but then nodded. "All right. I can do that."

She breathed a sigh of relief. Her name was close enough to Ana he hadn't questioned it. "Arthur," she began again, "where will we take them?"

"I have an idea, but it will mean leaving Germany. They might not like it when we return."

Anya could handle anything as long as the children would make it out of the country safe. "All right," she agreed.

"You haven't even heard my plan." He tilted his head to the side. "We will be alone for days, and your fiancé won't like that you've run away with another man."

She gagged. "Dierk can go to the Devil for all I care."

"Why are you marrying him if you don't like him?" he asked softly. His expression remained blank. Why did he even care if she married Dierk?

"We can discuss this all on the way to where we are going." She gestured toward the car. "Don't we need to leave?"

"You're right," he agreed. "But I expect you to answer me."

"I know," she said. "And I will."

They hurried and got inside. Mr. Jones—Arthur started the engine, and they took off. She hoped they made it out of the city without incident. Though once they managed to escape the main danger, the questions would start, and she didn't feel comfortable answering them all…

CHAPTER NINE

They were still driving well past daylight. Anya couldn't say how long they had been traveling. She didn't have a watch to check the time, and she had never been one to gauge the time by the rising of the sun. It didn't matter though. It could have been an hour or five, and her anxiety level still would not have leveled off.

Silence had filled the car the entire time Arthur had been driving. She had expected him to ask her a lot of questions. He had surely acted as if he would before they'd left. Now that he hadn't, it made her a thousand times more nervous. Why hadn't he said anything? Was he waiting for her to start speaking? Should she tell him everything? Somehow, she doubted he would understand her situation. She barely did, and she was living it.

"Are you going to tell me where we are going?" Anya couldn't take the never-ending quiet any longer. She'd never been the sort to sit still and enjoy the calm. That wouldn't change no matter what body she inhabited.

"You decided it was time to talk." He tapped the steering wheel. "It took a whole two hours. I'm amazed it took so long."

Two hours? She wouldn't have guessed it had been that long. How had he been able to keep track of the time? Should she ask that too? "You could have said something sooner if it bothered you." Now she was starting to get snippy. It was probably from lack of sleep, and hunger. Her stomach growled on cue.

"You told me you would explain everything on the way." His lips tilted downward, but he kept his focus on the road. That was probably a good thing. She had no desire to be in a car accident. "I am letting you control the pace. I suspect what you have to say is not easy to discuss with anyone."

She hadn't realized she was that transparent. "There isn't much to say." Anya shrugged noncommittally. "My father." She had a hard time referring to Edward Wegner as anyone related to her. "Wanted me to marry Dierk. I'm not in a position to deny him anything."

"But you don't even like him." He sounded exasperated as he spoke. "Why don't you put up a fight even if it is a token one."

How could she answer that? She didn't know what Anastasia had done. Had she protested the match, or had she gone willingly to the slaughter? Anya would have screamed and cried and begged until her father relented. The difference was Anya's father was a normal human who actually cared for her. They had a good relationship, and she could rely on him to protect her and care for her if needed. She missed him terribly... Anastasia's father was a controlling misogynistic arse who didn't care about anyone except himself and his own ambitions. "How do you know I didn't?" she said softly. "Or if I did that, it would matter? What good is a token effort if it ends with pain you cannot imagine?"

She had a feeling that Edward Wegner believed in physical punishment. He was harsh with her whenever they had to spend any amount of time together. She hadn't wanted to feel the sting of a slap or anything worse, so she had remained quiet and pretended to be a demure and obedient daughter.

When they returned, she might not be able to escape that type of punishment.

The muscles in Arthur's jaw tightened. Had she made him angry? She closed her eyes and took a deep breath. She hated this. What could she say to make this all right? Somehow, she didn't think the words existed, and she honestly didn't know if she cared.

"We should get married before we return," he said. His voice had no emotion in it as if he stated a fact that could not be disputed.

"Married?" She couldn't have heard him correctly.

"Yes," he confirmed.

"How is that going to solve anything?" Anya couldn't marry him. She could still return to her time. and when Anastasia woke up married to him, she would be horrified. She didn't have to know Anastasia to understand that. Anya wouldn't want anyone making that huge of a decision for her. "That would make everything so much worse."

"It won't," he insisted. "We need a reason for you to be gone for so long. They will have already sounded the alarm, and then they'll notice I am gone too. Naturally, they'll assume we are together. There is only one reason we would have left together that is acceptable. If they discover what we have really been doing, we might not live to see another day."

Well, when he put it like that... "You think they would kill us?" What was she saying? Of course they would. They'd do it and not think twice about it. The Nazis were committing genocide—one man and woman helping two Jewish children would be nothing compared to that. "Oh, God, why did I do this."

"Because you have a good heart," he said softly. "Those children needed help, and you didn't think about how that would affect you. Don't be hard on yourself."

"I had no plan and no clue what I was doing. I'd already be dead if I was on my own. If you hadn't found me..."

"I was already planning on helping the children," he said. "This is what I do. They don't watch me as much as they do you. I could have driven to Poland and back with none of them the wiser."

"Is that where we are going?" Poland was safe right now, but it wouldn't stay that way. In 1939, Germany would invade Poland and take over. The Jews there would be targeted. "The children can't stay there. They need to go to the States." That was the only place she believed they would truly be safe.

She would have suggested home if she was anyone other than Anastasia Wegner. To Arthur, the Americans were home to both of them. That would make sense…

"Do you think that is necessary?" he lifted a brow.

"Yes," she said. "They won't stop with Germany. They'll reach a point where the power consumes them, and they will want to control the world. They're extremist that believe they are righteous."

He was quiet for several moments. "I can see that happening. I'll make arrangements for them to go to my family in California. They'll keep them protected."

That was all she could hope for. This wouldn't all be for nothing if the children made it out alive. Anastasia might wake up one day married to Arthur, but that would be far better than being married to Dierk. "Good. Then I'll agree to whatever you think is necessary." Even if she didn't quite like it… She hated making decisions that would affect Anastasia's life. Anya prayed she was not making a mistake. There was no turning back now though. She couldn't change it even if she wanted to. Besides, Arthur was a good man. Anastasia would be far better off with him and she couldn't feel bad about that.

The children were safe. They had made it to Kostrzyn, Poland and were finally able to let the children out of the hidden part of the car. They hadn't dared while they were still in Germany. The entire trip had taken almost three hours. Arthur hadn't wanted to drive too fast and gain any unwanted notice. After they dropped Oskar and Johanna off with a lovely Polish family and arranged for them to travel to California, they had left. They didn't look back once. They did their duty, and that was all they could do.

After that, Arthur drove them to the nearest registry office in Poland for them to get married. They filed the necessary paperwork and waited for it to be approved, then made an appointment for a civil ceremony. The wedding was a blur and nothing like she had ever imagined. She was still dressed head to toe in black, and men's clothing to boot. Anya's attire suited a funeral more than a wedding.

"You won't regret this," Arthur said breaking the silence. "I won't treat you the way your father or Dierk does. If you don't want to stay married, we can have it dissolved when we return home to the States."

That was a small comfort…

"You don't want to stay married?" she asked. Anya had gotten the feeling he cared for her, or Anastasia. She couldn't be certain which considering she had no idea what their previous relationship had been like.

"I didn't say that," he said carefully. "I don't want you to feel obliged to honor our vows. We didn't say them under normal circumstances."

He tapped the steering wheel. The sky had grown dark and they were almost to the German border. They would soon discover what their fate would be when they returned. Would Dierk or Edward make her life miserable? Would she be able to escape the embassy altogether?

"We shouldn't stay here," she said quietly. "We will want to help, and it will become too difficult to hide our activities. I wish I could stop it all, but it is impossible. What is meant to be will be."

"You want to return home now?" he asked, surprise evident in her tone. "I thought you'd want to stay longer."

She shook her head. Anya would like nothing more than to return home…to her real home, but that wasn't possible. For whatever reason, fate had decided she needed to travel to the past. Was she supposed to learn some sort of life lesson? She couldn't be certain. "There's nothing to keep me here." That much was the truth anyway.

"Then we will go," he told her. "I will do whatever it is you want."

That sounded like a man in love. "Why are you helping me?" She had to understand his motives. Maybe if she did she could wrap her head around the entire situation.

The muscles in his cheek twitched. Had she hit a nerve? Did he not want to admit how he felt? She could relate to that. It was difficult for her to open up to anyone. Finally, he took a deep breath and started speaking. "There's something about you I cannot resist, never have been able to. You have an innocence about you that is refreshing in this harsh world. I want to protect you. Is that so wrong?"

Not an admission of love, but it might as well have been. She wasn't sure how it made her feel. Did he have feelings for her or Ana? She'd never truly know and that bothered her more than she wanted to admit. Did she want his love? Anya wasn't certain; however, she did care about him and he seemed to care for her. That would have to be enough. "I suppose so."

"What the hell is that?" He frowned. Anya turned her attention to the road and the blaring lights that greeted them outside the windshield.

"That wasn't there before…" It had been nothing but darkness until a moment ago. "They didn't want us to know they were there before." She barely managed to say the words. Anya had a very bad feeling…

"We should turn around and go back," he said. Arthur must have realized what they were about to face too.

Anya glanced behind her and nearly screamed. "We can't. There's no place to go." There were lights behind them too. They were cornered. "We're married now. They don't know what we did."

How could they? Did the Allendorfs betray them to save themselves? Anything was possible… Anya feared they might be doomed, but prayed she was wrong.

Arthur stopped the car and clenched the steering wheel. "Stay here," he ordered. "If something happens…" He paused and took a deep breath. "Slide over to the driver seat and try to go around them.

Do whatever you can to escape. Go back to where we took Oskar and Johanna. They'll help you."

"No…" she called to him, but he didn't stop. He slid out of the car and held his hands up as he walked toward the group on the road. Anya's heart beat heavily inside her chest, and she forgot how to breathe. Why was he walking toward them as if he didn't have any reason to be afraid? This was not going to end well. Somehow, she managed to push air into her lungs, but it burned with each breath. Her hands shook and her stomach was tied in knots.

Slowly, she raised her trembling hand and opened the car door, ready to go after him. She opened her mouth to tell him to come back, but nothing came out. He didn't even get halfway when one of them raised their gun and shot him. Anya screamed and did the very thing he told her not to do. She got out of the car and ran to him.

"Go back," he wheezed out the words. Blood pooled around his lips. "Stay safe."

"I can't leave you," her voice wobbled as she spoke. "Don't ask me to." A tear fell down her cheek and she barely contained her emotions.

"I lo…" He didn't finish the words before he stopped breathing. He was dead, and Anya had never been angrier in her life. She wiped the tears away and stood, then marched toward the German soldiers. They would take her back to the embassy, to her father, and she would make them pay for what they had done to her husband.

"Hello, dear," Dierk said then sneered. "My little whore."

She gasped. That was not what she'd been expecting. He was the trigger-happy soldier... He had meant to kill Arthur. She held her chin high. "I'm not whore."

"Perhaps not," he said. "But you are also no longer worthy." He lifted his pistol and aimed it at her. It was then she realized her mistake. He never intended for either one of them to make it out of this alive. Somehow, he had known there was something between Anastasia and Arthur. There was no other explanation. He must have been watching them both and decided to catch them in the act of betraying him. Anya had doomed them both. It was her fault Arthur was dead, and soon she would be too.

"You can't shoot me. The embassy..."

"Will think you ran away with your lover and stop looking for you. Don't worry, dear, I'll make it quick. I might have sampled your favors first, but I don't want used goods."

Anya took several steps backward, intending to

try to run to the car. She should have listened to Arthur. She didn't make it far before the blast of a gunshot echoed through the air and the sting of pain filled her. She fell backward and landed next to Arthur. She coughed, and blood spurted from her mouth and trailed down her cheek. She was dying. Anya had made one mistake too many, and the cost had been great. Arthur was dead. Ana would be dead. Her fate...she didn't know, but she perhaps she deserved that uncertainty. She'd been foolish. Dierk moved forward and stopped to leer over her. "Good-bye, love," he said maniacally, then aimed and fired one last time.

CHAPTER TEN

*T*he pain reverberated through her skull, and it almost felt a little like déjà vu. The tiny hammers happily pounding against Anya's skull in thousands of different places had to go. The bloody devils seemed particularly focused on her forehead above her eyes. She was afraid to open her eyelids for fear of what she might discover. What happened to her? She couldn't remember how she'd hurt herself, and she wasn't certain she wanted to.

Then she remembered, and her eyelids flew open. Bright light greeted her along with the gentle *beep, beep* of a nearby monitor. The room was stark white with soft yellow highlights. It wasn't her bedchamber, or Anastasia's, it looked like a hospital room. A simple room with a little space and not much to offer it.

"You're awake," a female said suddenly. Her voice was warm and comforting. "You had us so worried. Your mother will be ecstatic."

Anya turned toward the sound of the voice. She blinked several times to bring the person into focus. "Lorelei?" Her cousin sat near the bed, knitting a blanket. Her cinnamon red hair was pulled back away from her face at the sides, but the rest of it hung at her shoulder in waves, and her hazel eyes held a warmth similar to the tone of her voice.

"Where am I?" She tried to sit up and groaned. She'd been shot. Anya clearly remembered Dierk pointing the gun at her head and firing, but that had been Anastasia. He'd killed her, and it had returned her home... She had been hurt, but somehow she doubted her wounds were from a gun. "What happened?"

"You poor dear," Lorelei said. "You really don't remember?" She put her knitting needles together and folded the blanket and then shoved it all into a nearby tote. "There was an accident at the event. Something about a clumsy boy and some boxes. I'm not entirely certain how it all happened, but you hit your head hard, and you've been in a coma for a few weeks."

"Weeks?" She gasped. In a weird way that almost made sense. "I…" She swallowed hard and took a deep breath.

"I'm so sorry," Lorelei told her. "I'll go get a nurse. The doctor will want to check on you now that you're awake. I'll also call your parents. You know how your mama frets."

She was out of the room before Anya could stop her. Her mother meant well, but she could be difficult. She'd rather her mother stayed away until she was able to acclimate to her surroundings. It all had seemed so real, but she'd been in a coma the entire time. How had she imagined it all? They were all people she hadn't known or even heard their names before her weird coma induced dream. Though there had been one person there she'd met previously—Lady Vivian. Perhaps she should explore that. It could be that Lady Vivian had mentioned some of the individuals from her dream.

"I hear someone is awake," a woman said as she entered the room. She wore a full white apron over an indigo dress. Her ebony locks were pulled back into a ponytail and she had eyes so blue they were almost eerie. "I'm your nurse. You can call me Sara."

"Hello," Anya said a little apprehensively. The nurse was way too perky. "When can I leave?"

She chuckled lightly. "You woke up a little while ago. I'm not so certain you're leaving until the doctor has a chance to check on you. You're here at the very least until tomorrow when he does his rounds."

Anya didn't want to wait that long. She hated hospitals, and she wanted to be home, and crawl into her own bed. Maybe once she was there she'd find it comforting and she could forget the trauma of living someone else's life. A bang echoed through the room, and she jumped from the sound.

"Easy," Sara said soothingly as she placed her hand on Anya's shoulder. "Someone dropped a metal tray. It happens."

Her hand shook a little as she lifted it to Sara's and removed it from her shoulder. She didn't want her comfort. It felt wrong somehow. Everything inside of her screamed as if something was missing and she could never find it again. If she closed her eyes, she could see Dierk pointing his gun at her and squeezing the trigger.

It had seemed so real, and the pain...it had been equally intense. Almost as if she had actually felt it as she bled out on the pavement. If it had really happened though…then both Arthur and Ana were dead. Somehow, she'd survived, but they would still be gone forever. That hurt more than she liked. Tears threatened to fall from her eyes, but she swallowed the agony. Now was not the time to give in to her emotional chaos.

"I'm all right." She glanced away, not wanting the nurse to see how unsettled that sound had actually made her. It had reminded her of the gunshot, and it had been almost as if that pain hit her again. It was like she had lived through that experience, and it hadn't been the dream she believed it to be.

"I don't believe you, but I'll let you keep your secrets, for now," Sara told her. "I'll get your vitals and leave you in peace. I suspect your family will descend upon you soon enough. They've all been worried about you."

She feared the nurse was right. "I'm sorry if they've been difficult."

"Not at all." Sara waved her hand. "They love you and that is always good to witness." She gestured toward Anya's wrist. "If you don't mind, I'd like to check your pulse."

Anya lifted her wrist. The sooner the nurse

finished she'd leave. Of course, once her parents arrived, she wouldn't have any peace for some time to come. She didn't blame them. If she had a child and they were in a coma for weeks, she'd be worried too, and if she hadn't been through a trauma she might be more sympathetic.

The nurse finished taking her vitals and wrote them down in the chart. "All done." She smiled. "If you need anything, do not be afraid to call."

"Thank you," she said. Her throat was a little parched, but she didn't want to ask the nurse for anything. She wanted a little bit of quiet before her mother and father showed up. Lorelei would still be around too. She'd left her knitting bag on the floor next to the chair. Her cousin wouldn't want to leave that behind.

The nurse nodded and left her alone. She had a few minutes at least until chaos descended...

Anya stared out the window, wishing she was outside. She was leaving the hospital finally. The doctor had kept her three days past the day she'd woken up. She was itching to escape. Sleep had evaded her, and when she did close her eyes, images of Arthur's death plagued her. She had to find out if he was real, if Anastasia existed, and if they had really died so tragically. She hadn't loved Arthur, but Anastasia might have. Anya might have fallen for him if she'd had time. She had cared for him. He was brave and had helped her through her own foolishness. If there ever was a man she could have loved, it would have been him. She owed it to them to uncover their story, and she knew exactly where to begin her search.

"Are you ready, dear?" Her mother asked. Eleanor Montgomery, the Countess of Parkdale's dark blonde hair was cropped short and framed her face. She wore an elegant burgundy suit that hugged her slim frame.

"I've been ready for days," she answered. "Where's Father?"

"He went to get the car." She smiled. "You know how he is. He can't sit still."

Anya didn't blame her father. She didn't want to be in the hospital either. She had to start her search. In order to do that, she had to talk to her boss. Lady Vivian might remember Anastasia, and after she talked to her, she would know where to go next.

"I hear someone is leaving us today." Nurse Sara walked into the room. She had a cheery smile on her face that irritated Anya. The nurse had been nice and helpful, so Anya didn't understand why she found Sara irritating. She was surly, and it had nothing to do with the nurse. "I have your discharge papers." Sara held out a stack of papers. "After you sign them, you're free to go. Well, you will need to ride in a wheelchair downstairs. Hospital policy, sorry."

Anya wrinkled her nose. "Fine. Give me the papers." She took the stack from Sara and flipped to the signature page, picked up a pen, then scribbled her name across the line. "There."

"I'll have someone come in with the wheelchair soon." Sara grabbed the papers. "Do you have any questions before I leave?"

"No," Anya shook her head. She didn't want to delay that wheelchair's arrival. Without it, she couldn't escape, and she desperately needed to depart the bloody hospital.

"All right," she said. "Then relax, and you'll be out of here before you know it."

Anya sank into the nearby chair. She reminded herself that this was an obstacle she could surpass. Nothing would stand in her way in search of the truth. It was a minor delay, nothing more.

"I know you're frustrated," her mother said. "It could be worse."

"Could it?" She frowned. "I suppose so. I could be dead."

"What a morbid thing to say," her mother chastised her. "Why would you even suggest…" Her hand shook, and she brought it up to her chest. "Do you have any idea how scared we were? You were so hurt…"

"I'm fine," Anya said dryly. She should have known better than to be that blunt with her mother. "Please accept my apologies. I didn't mean to upset you." That was the truth. She hadn't taken her mother's feelings into account at all. When Anya thought about her own death, she pictured a gun going off clearly in her mind. She had died and knew what it was like to take her last breath. That wasn't something she was likely to ever forget.

"This has been difficult for you," her mother said gently. "You have a good heart. In time, your stress will ease, and this will be a distant memory."

Would it though? Somehow, she doubted she'd ever forget this experience. "It was an accident." Her voice remained monotone as she spoke. Anya was going through the motions.

"I'm here to take Anya Montgomery downstairs?" A woman came in with a wheelchair. She had on a pink sweater and navy-blue trousers. She was close to her mother's age. Her auburn hair was pulled back behind her head in a simple braid. "I am Catherine, Marchioness of Seabrook." She winked. "I usually do not announce that tidbit, but I thought you should know. It's something you might contemplate over later. I'm a nurse, but these days I volunteer here at the hospital."

That was interesting… Why had she worked at all if she was a marchioness? The volunteering part made sense. Most high society ladies did some sort of charity work, but why did she feel the need to disclose her title to her? Why would Anya ever need to know that?

"That would be me," Anya said as she raised her hand. "I'm ready to go. Are you really a marchioness?" Perhaps she was lying? Though she didn't understand why.

"I am, but let's forego the formalities, shall we? I'd much prefer you use my given name, Catherine. I've never much cared to be called Lady Seabrook," the woman told her, then patted the chair. "Hop in and we'll get you home."

She got up and then sat down in the wheelchair. The woman walked backward and turned the chair around to push it out of the room. "They've come a long way with these chairs. My husband had to use one when he was injured in the first world war. It was a big bulky thing."

"A marquess fought in the war?" She didn't think they did that. Her mother walked beside the wheelchair as they moved through the hall. She remained quiet. Anya had upset her more than she thought. She'd have to apologize again later.

"He was a spy. We met before the war started and fell in love through the years as it raged on. We married and returned home before the war ended."

"Because he was injured?"

Anya didn't know why she was curious. It helped her a little to hear about a story of love that survived. The woman had to be in her fifties. Anya wanted a love like that. One that would stand the test of time and survive well past the hard times.

"He was," she said. "Asher could no longer be a spy, at least not effectively anymore. We also had to bring the twins, my son and daughter, home before it became impossible to do so. They were mere infants when we left." They would probably be around the same age as Lady Vivian. She'd been born during the first world war too.

"Thank you for sharing your story with me." It had given Anya something to consider.

"I thought it might help you," she said softly. "I could feel your distress."

That was odd too... How would she have any idea what Anya was feeling? Though she had been irritable. Perhaps she had given off some sort of signs she hadn't been aware of.

"Here we are," Catherine said. "It was nice meeting you." She leaned down and whispered, "Don't be afraid of your gifts. They'll guide you where you need to go. Trust yourself." After she finished speaking, she pushed the chair to the end of the pavement. "I believe that is your father. Enjoy your visit to Weston."

Anya stood from the chair and turned to speak to her, but Catherine was already backing the chair away and returning to the hospital. Was Lady Vivian at Weston? How had Catherine known she needed to find her? She could be reading too much into it, but somehow she didn't think so. Instead of going after her, she got into the car. She didn't have any time to waste.

"She's always been strange," her mother said. "Don't pay her any mind. She may be a marchioness, but she lacks class."

Anya rolled her eyes. Her mother was probably jealous Catherine had a better title than her. She would ignore her comment, but she might try to find Catherine again one day. She couldn't wait to get to her place. As soon as her parents left her flat, she fully intended to leave and drive to Weston; she'd have to finally purchase a car first. She had to see Lady Vivian.

CHAPTER ELEVEN

*A*nya hadn't been able to leave London as soon as she would have liked. It was probably for the best that she'd been waylaid though. After she'd walked into her flat, she'd felt faint and had to lie down...a condition that was not conducive to traveling. Especially since she fully intended to drive herself to Dover. After a few days of convalescence, she packed a bag for her trip, then left her flat to secure transportation. She carried her small bag with her to catch the next double-decker. Anya didn't want to return to retrieve it after her car-buying spree.

She knew exactly what kind of car she wanted. Anya had thought about it for a while, but hadn't bought it because she had deemed the expenditure frivolous. Now, though, she didn't care. After almost dying in the present, and actually dying in the past, she made the decision to live her life to the fullest. Anya still wasn't certain her dream had been real, but she could still feel the pain from being shot. That was real enough for her to make different decisions for her life. When the double-decker arrived, she stepped on with purpose. Nothing would distract her from her goal.

As the bus moved through the London streets, it gave Anya time to think about what she'd ask Lady Vivian when she found her in Dover. Asking her outright about her time with Anastasia Wegner might raise questions she didn't really want to answer. She wasn't certain how to explain why it mattered to her. Lady Vivian would believe her mad if she told her the truth. It was best to keep that part of her coma experience to herself. Dealing with the aftermath already made her a nervous wreck. Any sudden movements or loud sounds and she nearly jumped out of her skin. It would take her a long while not to react that way. Sometimes it seemed as if she'd truly been shot and killed. That was not something she'd reconcile herself with any time soon, if ever.

The bus came to a stop and jolted her out of her

own mind. She glanced out the window and sighed. Time to go shopping. She stood and made her way off the double-decker and stepped on to the pavement. It was a few blocks to the dealership. She hoped it wouldn't be too difficult to buy a car for immediate use. If she had to, she'd throw her father's name around. Telling people she was the daughter of the Earl of Parkdale opened many doors. She didn't do it often, only in extreme emergencies. Which she deemed this to be...

It was exhausting to do almost anything after her stint in the hospital. If her parents were aware of her excursion, they'd likely try to stop her. She couldn't allow that to happen. When she walked into the building, no one immediately came to her aid. That disappointed her. They probably didn't think helping her would result in an instantaneous sale.

"Hello," she called out. "Is anyone available to help me make a purchase?"

An older gentleman turned toward her and lifted a brow. He seemed to mock her with that gesture. Anya pursed her lips in displeasure and tapped her foot anxiously. Two could play that game... She'd be more than happy to be snootier than him. He brushed his fingers over the side of his silver-tipped dark hair and sighed. Of course, he gave in first and approached her. "How may I assist you?"

"I'd like to buy an Aston Martin. Bright red if it's available, but I'm open to whatever you have on hand for me to drive away with today."

"An Aston Martin?" The astonishment in his tone echoed around her. As if, *how dare you try to buy something inappropriate for you little girl...*

"Yes," she said and lifted her chin defiantly. "What do you have available?"

"Are you certain that is the car you wish to own?" He stared down at her as if trying to will her to make a different decision. "It's…not a car for a woman."

She'd had enough of male chauvinism to last a lifetime. Not to mention Ana's controlling father and fiancé from her messed up dream reality. No man would dictate to her ever again, real or imagined. "Who are you to tell me what I can or cannot buy?" She glared at him. "I want an Aston Martin, and I shall have one." Anya reverted to the spoiled child she'd been before learning humility. "Perhaps you'd rather deal with my father, Lord Parkdale."

"That won't be necessary," he said quickly. He waved his hand frantically, and he seemed a little anxious after she dropped her father's name. *Good.* "I only have one Aston Martin, but I can show it to you if you'd like. I'm afraid it isn't red…"

Anya waved her hand dismissively. She really did not care about the color. She'd thought it sounded better to demand something. "That's fine. Show it to me."

The man took her to the car and allowed her to look it over. It wasn't a convertible, which was too bad…she'd have liked one, but she'd make do. It was a silvery blue that she loved. Red would have been fun, but this suited her more. It actually reminded her of Arthur's eyes. That sent a stab of pain through her heart, but she suppressed it. Now wasn't the time to think about a past that wasn't actually hers.

"I'll take it."

"You don't wish to drive it?" the older man asked, a little baffled.

"I'll drive it after I've purchased it. There's no need to do so before. I trust there's nothing wrong with a brand-new automobile?" She lifted a brow.

"No, of course not," he reassured her. "Come with me, and we will start the paperwork."

Anya let out a deep breath she hadn't realized she'd been holding. The man probably thought her odd, but she couldn't bring herself to care. He could think she was addled, and it wouldn't matter. As long as the sale of the car went through, she'd be fine at the end of it. She didn't anticipate there would be any issues, but it was better to be prepared for the worst.

It took almost too long to fill out all the paperwork and pay for the car, and she hadn't foreseen that it would. Once she had the keys in her hand, she placed her bag in the passenger seat and started for Dover. It would take her almost two hours to arrive at Weston Manor. She didn't want to delay for any reason.

ANYA HAD a lot of time to think on her drive to Dover. She relived every moment she'd spent with Arthur, from the opera, to the museum, to their wedding. All of it was surreal…as if she were watching a movie on the screen. It might even make a good movie for the world to see. Perhaps, once she had Anastasia's story, all of it, she'd write a script. Lady Vivian might consider producing it at the Film Institute. It was worth considering anyway.

She pulled into a petrol station. Anya hadn't intended to stop, but her tank was running low. Canterbury was an interesting town with its own history. She might stop and spend a little time there on her return trip to London. Anya didn't have the time to dawdle now. She had a mission to complete, and that meant continuing on to Weston Manor. She prayed Lady Vivian was still in residence. It would be irritating if she had left once she arrived. Catherine had indicated she should go to Weston with her cryptic message. She hadn't taken her word for it though. She had called the institute to inquire, and they said Lady Vivian had gone on holiday and wouldn't return for three weeks. That meant she would have to go looking for her.

An attendant came out to the gas pump. He had red hair that reminded her of Catherine, but was on the thinner side. His eyes were so blue they almost seemed black. He was a striking young man, and she couldn't help thinking he might be related to the marchioness. That couldn't be right though. A relative of hers wouldn't work at a petrol station. "You need a fill up?" he asked.

"Yes, please," she said.

He pulled the handle on the pump and started to fill her tank. He washed her windows and then finished putting the petrol into her car. She handed him several pounds to cover the cost. "Keep the change," she told him.

"Much obliged," he said and nodded at her. "Drive safely."

She started the engine and pulled away from the pumps, then drove on to the road. It wouldn't take long before she reached Weston. She'd never been to the manor house on the cliffs of Dover, but she'd heard it was gorgeous. In some ways, she was glad to have a reason to visit the estate.

Thirty minutes later, she turned down the long driveway that led to Weston Manor. She stopped outside the main entrance and put her car into park. She frowned. Now that she'd arrived, she suddenly felt unsure. Would she be welcomed? Would Lady Vivian be irritated with her for presuming it was all right to show up at her family home? Anya took a deep breath and then prepared to go inside. She left her bag on the front seat. She would not presume she'd be a welcome visitor. She'd drive into town and find a hotel later.

She pushed open the door to her car and stepped out. After a moment, she forced herself to close it and head to the entrance. She lifted the knocker and rapped it several times. It didn't take long before a butler opened the large wooden door and said, "Yes?" He held his head high. He was the butler to a duke, after all. "How may I help you?"

"I wish to see Lady Vivian," she said.

He nodded. "Are you Lady Anya Montgomery?"

She tilted her head to the side, confused. Anya hadn't called ahead to let them know she was coming. How could the butler possibly know her name? "I am," she said slowly.

"Do you have your luggage?"

Anya stood completely still. This was not going at all how she'd expected. At best, she hoped for an audience with Lady Vivian. If she were invited to stay, even better. She did not, once, believe they would anticipate her arrival. "I have one bag in my front seat."

"Very well," the butler said. "Give me your keys, and I'll see that your suitcase is taken to your room and your car stored in the garage." He held out his hand and she slid her car key into it. "Now, follow me. Tea is being served in the salon. The duchess and Lady Vivian are already there."

Wonderful. She'd wanted to have a pointed conversation with Lady Vivian, but how could she do that with her mother there too? At least Anya was able to stay at the manor even though it was odd that they already planned on having her there. Did they have some sort of premonition that she'd be coming?

Anya frowned. Perhaps Catherine had informed

them. She had told her to enjoy her visit at Weston. From what she could recall, the Seabrooks and Westons were close…perhaps even distantly related. It wouldn't be too much of a stretch to believe Catherine had warned them she'd suddenly arrive on their doorstep.

The butler bowed, then announced, "Lady Anya Montgomery."

"Come in," the duchess waved at her. "You must be parched after your long journey." Anya had known the duchess was an American, but her accent still threw her off. It was sweet, and distinctive, like a true Southern belle. Of course it shouldn't have startled her, at least not because it was so different than her own, or Lady Vivian's. If Anya's dream was actually real, and she had started to believe it had been, then she'd met the duchess in the past as Ana. Her voice was similar, but her face had aged slightly, as it should have in the years since the war.

Lady Vivian sipped on her tea. "How are you, dear? I've been worried about you."

Not enough to visit her in the hospital… Perhaps she was being too harsh. Lady Vivian could have visited her while she was still in a coma. "I'm well enough." She didn't want to discuss her health.

"Good," she said. "Now do as my mother bade

127

you. Come sit. You were released from the hospital mere days ago. You shouldn't overtax yourself."

Anya ambled over to a nearby chair and sat down. The duchess poured her a cup of tea. "How do you take it?"

"One sugar please," she told her. The duchess put the sugar into the cup and then handed it to her. She sipped it mostly because she didn't know what else to do. What should she say or do? This wasn't what she had planned, and she didn't know what her next action should be. "Thank you."

Neither of them spoke. Anya sighed and then sipped her tea again. The door to the salon opened, and a gentleman walked in. He had dark hair, a little on the longer side, and blue eyes very much similar to the shade Arthur's had been. Pain, guilt, and something close to longing stung her heart. Those feelings were almost too much to bear. She shook the image from her mind. This was *not* Arthur. She didn't know who he was, but she understood that much.

"It's about time," Lady Vivian said. "We've been waiting for you."

"Welcoming as always, sister dear," the gentleman said as he moved into the room with almost graceful movements. She didn't' know how else to explain it.

He stopped in front of her and she lifted her gaze to meet his. His lips tilted upward into a devilish smile that stole her heart. It seemed familiar somehow. She then realized then the identity of the man. This was Mathias, the Marquess of Blackthorn, Lady Vivian's younger brother. "I'm glad you are finally here." He held out his hand to her. "Will you come walk with me?"

Anya stared down at his outstretched hand in confusion. Should she take it? What did he mean to show her? Why did he want to spend time with her? They had never met before this moment...well, not as Anya anyway. She'd seen him in her dream when she inhabited Anastasia's body. Not to mention she was a little annoyed that she had to wait to talk to Vivian. That had been her sole reason for making the trip to Weston. Now Vivian's brother wanted her to spend time with him instead? That was...odd.

"My apologies," he began. "It's not my intention to frighten you." She jerked her head upward and narrowed her gaze. That statement sounded too familiar and made her leery—she'd heard it some- where before... She slowly put her hand in his. It was time to end this charade and uncover what was really going on. If it meant spending some time with Lord Blackthorn, so be it.

CHAPTER TWELVE

nya didn't understand why or how she managed to engulf herself in situations that were questionable. If she, as Anastasia, hadn't felt the need to do her part to save the world, she may not have been shot and killed. Though she still wondered if that was a figment of her imagination or not. How could it have been real? She needed some evidence to prove to her it; until then, she'd never fully accept it. If it had been, then she'd done the right thing. The children had been saved and hopefully lived a full life. Surely that had been worth the pain and suffering she'd endured to make that happen.

She shook those thoughts away because she had to focus on her present and where Mathias, Lord

Blackthorn, was leading her. He hadn't let go of her hand as they walked through Weston Manor, leading her into a large library with several books lining the shelves. Some of them appeared quite old...

A large mirror with ornate scrollwork down the sides called to her, and she couldn't explain why; it seemed special. As if touching it would take her places she could only imagine, but hadn't she done enough of that inside her own head? Anya had no desire to visit anywhere more exotic than England and the time she currently resided in. As far as she was concerned, her adventuring days were done. She forced herself to glance away from it and turn her attention to the elusive man beside her. Anya faced him and asked, "Why did you want me to come in here with you?"

He shoved his hands into his pockets and lifted his lips into a devastating smile. It turned her insides to liquid, and it embarrassed her how much he affected her. She'd just met him...this older version of him. "You don't have much patience, do you?"

"If it is warranted, I can have an endurance that far outlasts anything you could imagine." She tilted her chin upward. "My fortitude is boundless, but that doesn't have anything to do with the here and now. I let you lead me here, and now I expect you to answer some of my questions."

"Only some?" He lifted a brow.

"Are we using semantics now?" She rolled her eyes. He was delaying answering her for some reason. She didn't want to play these games with him. "I suppose I should consider there are some questions that might be to uncomfortable for you to answer, but that doesn't mean I'm going to abstain from asking them." She folded her arms over her chest. "Now. Let's start with an easy one: why did you expect me to come here? You still have not told me what you want from me. How many times do I have to ask."

"As many as it takes?" His lips twitched. "I agree that is perhaps the simplest question, as is its answer, but I suspect you already know."

She narrowed her gaze. "You've mastered answering questions without actually giving infor-mation away. That's almost...spy worthy. Do you work with some government agency that specializes in espionage?"

"No," he replied and shook his head lightly. "Wrong branch of the family tree, so to speak. Though my father did act as a spy during the first world war, it is usually not a Kendall trait." He walked over to the shelf and pulled a book off. He started flipping through it. "You met Catherine, the Marchioness of Seabrook, correct?"

"I did." What was he saying with that question? Was he about to admit that she told him that Anya would arrive at Weston? "What of it?"

"Her husband and my father worked together in the war. Our family is related by several generations removed." He stopped and stared at one of the pages. "Catherine is special. She has...certain gifts."

"She mentioned she used to be a nurse," Anya offered. "Some believe nurses find it a calling."

He closed the book over his finger to mark his page and strolled over to her, carrying it. "Catherine has her reasons for becoming a nurse. She wanted to help and had a vision about the war. She's also...empathetic."

Empathy? She could feel a person's emotions? And did he say vision? "Uh huh," she replied noncommittally. If any of that was true, then Catherine must have known the turmoil inside of Anya's head. Had she had a vision of her? Could she know what had actually happened to her? She had considered finding Catherine again before, but now she really wanted to speak to her again. The entire thing made her incredibly uncomfortable, and she didn't have any idea what to make of it all. "What does this have to do with me, and why I am here?"

"She's the reason we knew when to expect you, but the reason you are here isn't answered so easily." He held the book to her. "Please read this."

She took it from him, ensuring she kept the page open to where he'd wanted her to read. It was a poem. That hadn't been what she'd expected. Anya kept her finger on the page and flipped back to the title of the book. A compilation of poetry by John Keats. Her heart skipped a beat. What were the chances he'd want her to read a poem by Arthur's favorite poet? What one had he chosen? She prayed it wasn't the same one Arthur had quoted from, if so, she might lose control of her emotions.

Anya flipped back and read the lines of the poem...the first one standing out to her—*"Bright star, would I were steadfast as thou art"*— Not the same poem. She was grateful for that, but still confused. "Why did you wish for me to read this?"

"You like poetry, do you not?" He took the book from her. "This poem...like most of Keats's work, is extraordinary. He wrote it when he was facing his own death."

She frowned. "Are you dying?"

He chuckled. "No. I'm quite well. Are you

worried over my health?" He closed the book. "Never mind that." Lord Blackthorn tapped the book. "This book is about our mortality. Keats was staring up at the sky, wishing he could have their longevity, but didn't envy them for their lack of human warmth, the loneliness."

"That even in death in the end we accept our fate because we have those we love with us." She paraphrased what he was trying to say without understanding for one second why he brought up the topic.

"Yes," he smiled. "If we are fortunate enough, as we take our last breath, the love of our life is there beside us through it all."

"This poetry lesson has been fascinating." She closed her eyes and took a deep breath. She had to try to keep control. It wouldn't do anyone, especially her, any good to give in to any emotional upheaval. Her life had taken a strange turn. Mathias couldn't know that or what the poetry might mean to her. "But I must say it isn't the enlightenment I sought. Are you ready to have a real conversation?"

"Will you spend the day with me tomorrow?" he asked. Amusement echoed through his tone. It irritated her.

"I'm not certain that is wise." She waved her hand

dismissively. "This has been quite the useless endeavor."

"I disagree," he told her. "I've shared a great deal and learned more about you. You're not open to the information I presented to you, so it seems out of place. In time, the truth will be evident. Let me prove it to you." He moved closer to her. "Please spend the day with me."

Anya didn't feel as if she could say no. She wanted to, but… "All right," she said before she could stop herself. "I will."

ANYA STILL COULDN'T BELIEVE she'd agreed to this. She should never have allowed him to persuade her. Lord Blackthorn was not the reason she'd come to Weston. He waylaid her and distracted her from her true intentions. She should have gone in search of Lady Vivian again, but had reluctantly awaited the marquess in the foyer as he'd instructed before they departed the night. If he didn't make an appearance soon, she'd go with her first instinct and locate Lady Vivian, but she had to at least attempt to be patient.

She tapped her foot against the floor, belying her ability to remain anything remotely serene. Anya would never be able to disguise her pique and anxiety, and she had no particular desire to do so. Where was Lord Blackthorn? She blew out an exasperated breath and headed for the door. She couldn't take it anymore. Standing in the foyer reminded her too much of the embassy and the restrictions set on Anastasia. She had no wish to relive any of that experience. She opened the door and stepped one foot out.

"Are you in a hurry?" Lord Blackthorn asked in an affable tone.

Anya froze in the doorway, her hand still firmly clutched around the handle. He had rotten bloody timing. She eased her grip, let go of the doorknob and turned toward him. "My lord," she greeted him formally. "I suspected you decided upon a different engagement and chose to do so myself. My apologies for my presumption. Do you still wish to spend the day with me?" *Please say no.* She feared what the outcome of the day might prevail upon her. Something deep inside of her dreaded it.

"I must insist you not speak formally with me. No *my lords*, or *Lord Blackthorn*. I prefer Matt, but if that is too personal, then Mathias." His lips tilted upward into a wicked smile that sent every one of her nerve endings all aflutter. "We are not two souls forced into propriety because of nineteenth century standards. It is the twentieth century. I do believe we can loosen the rules a little."

When he put it like that… "All right, we can use our given names. It is a little ridiculous, I suppose. Please call me Anya then."

"Thank you," he paused a moment and then said her name in a much softer tone, "Anya." That made her all aflutter again. What was it about him saying her name that made her want to move closer, touch him, and so much more. She barely restrained herself from acting upon the urge. "Now, shall we go?" He closed the distance between them and then held out his arm to her. Slowly, she looped her arm with his and allowed him to escort her outside.

"What have you planned for us?"

"We're not doing anything extravagant." His tone was jovial as he spoke. "I do hope you don't find that disappointing. I thought we'd spend the day here on the grounds. There is much I'd like to show you, and even more I'd like to tell you, if you'll allow it."

"I agreed to spend the day with you. I'm not about to go back on my word now." She tilted her chin upward. "As long as you're not untoward, that is."

"I promise I won't do anything that you don't agree to. I'd never take advantage of you."

Anya believed him. He'd been proper at every turn. The only thing he did against propriety was to insist on using their given names, and that was more normal today than it used to be once upon a time. "All right," she said. "I am all aquiver with eagerness at your plans. Do proceed." She didn't try to hide her lack of enthusiasm from her tone. Anya was a little bit curious, but that didn't mean she had to give in to it. Some things were better not known. She learned that lesson the hard way in a dream that was probably a reality she couldn't shake.

"You will be," he said. "But I understand that you're uncertain of everything right now."

He led her away from the house and they walked toward the cliffs. She didn't know anything about the Weston estate. When she arrived, she hadn't taken the time to look at her surroundings. It was beautiful. The sky was a mix of blue and purple, and she wanted to go to the edge to see the water below. That might be a little insane considering how much she hated heights, but she'd be willing to bet it was a gorgeous view.

"Our family's history is long and winding, like most families with our background," Mathias began.

"You understand, considering your father is the Earl of Parkdale."

"I do," she confirmed. There were many portraits at her family estate outlining her heritage. "Where are you going with this?"

He pointed to the cliffs. "One of my ancestors fell from that cliff." He turned to her and smiled. "She traveled through time, and then married James Kendall, the Duke of Weston that lived in 1815."

"Is that so?" It sounded fantastical to her. If he believed that, then it was possible that he might actually consider her story to be factual. "Do you expect me to believe that?"

"I do," he said. "Because it's the truth. In time, we're supposed to conceal that truth so one of my descendants is unaware of it. His lack of knowledge is essential to ensuring my ancestor does everything exactly the same so that we all exist. It's a weird paradox you see, because she's from the future."

"Uh huh," Anya didn't believe it for one second. "Why are we heading toward the cliffs." Why would he think she might? He couldn't possibly know about the dream she had about traveling back in time and inhabiting another person's body. Could he? If he believed a person could feel another's emotions or have visions, then anything was possible. With that line of thought, her experience could have actually happened to her as well. Mind boggling really…

"So we can go down to the beach."

She gasped. Had she heard him correctly? "Do you plan on jumping then?" She swallowed the lump in her throat. "Or push me?"

He chuckled. "I promised I wouldn't harm you. We're going down to the beach by less suicidal means; though I must warn you, the path can be slippery. I'll protect you as best I can. Are you willing to take that risk?"

Anya sighed. She'd already died in a dream; how much worse could this be? "I am," she agreed. He was a fount of knowledge, but she wasn't certain she understood why he imparted some of it. Perhaps, as the day went on, she'd uncover the truth. So she followed him down the path to the beach below, ready for anything.

CHAPTER THIRTEEN

*W*hen they reached the bottom of the path, Anya breathed a sigh of relief. He hadn't lied about the slipperiness. She was glad to be off it and didn't particularly look forward to the trek back. The beach was gorgeous, and Mathias had definitely planned ahead. A dark blanket had been laid out with a basket laying on top of it. Admittedly, she was curious what foods he had packed for their picnic, and she couldn't help being a little interested in him as well. She hadn't wanted a picnic alone with him, but now, she hoped to uncover some of his secrets. Why was he so insistent about spending time with her? What was his goal? She needed to understand him, and she couldn't fathom why.

"We will eat later. I wanted to walk with you on the beach for a little while first."

"I'm not particularly hungry at the moment, so that is all right with me." She was curious, and she'd follow along with his plans as long as she remained so.

He was silent for a while as they walked along the beach. Anya stopped to pick up a rock and skipped it across the waves as they rolled to the shore. She almost wished she had a bathing suit so she could swim. Maybe another time, if there was another one…

He stopped and stared out at the water. "I know you don't believe me about the time travel," he began. "I could prove it to you, but that part of my family's past doesn't pertain to you or me, not exactly."

What did his "not exactly" mean? How could it not pertain to them, but somehow it did? That made no sense. "Then why tell me that story?" She turned toward him and lifted a brow. She didn't understand Mathias, or why she was so drawn to him. She needed to know more, and then perhaps it would all make sense somehow.

"To warm you up to the idea," he said simply.

"The idea of its existence had to be a possibility to you for you to accept everything else."

She had thought she'd traveled through time while she was in a coma. Of course, she hadn't physically traveled, it had been her conscious that had done so. That wasn't even the truth. Her brain made up some weird story she had believed she lived through. She kept telling herself that, but she didn't really believe it. If she had, she'd never have left London and went searching for Lady Vivian.

But none of that had to do with anything Mathias was talking about. He believed his ancestor had traveled body and soul from a future they hadn't experienced to a past that they read about in history books. "And do you believe you were successful in gaining my acceptance of the possibility?"

"No," he replied easily. "You are still skeptical even though you've had an experience of a sort yourself."

He couldn't know about her dream coma. She hadn't told anyone about it. "Is that so?" She would not admit to anything. Anya didn't want anyone to think she was insane.

"Perhaps if I told you more of our history." He folded his hands behind his back and rocked on his heels. "Open up and lay it all out for you to decipher the truth."

"That would be refreshing," she answered. Though Anya wasn't sure she was capable of recognizing the difference between honesty and deceit. She was balancing over a very fine line, and she might topple over to one side easily.

"Do you recall me discussing Catherine and her gifts?"

How could she forget? It had been presumed that those gifts had allowed for them to expect Anya's arrival. Though she didn't quite understand the how or why to any of it. "You have yet to explain it all to me. If you recall, you distracted me with Keats."

Mathias chuckled. "That I did. I like Keats." Arthur had liked the poet too. That memory stung, and she closed her eyes to hold back tears. After the pain eased, she opened them again and did her best to keep her attention focused on Mathias.

"He's not my favorite," she admitted. "But he's tolerable."

"I know you're fond of Tennyson, if I recall."

She jerked back. How could he possibly know that? Anya hadn't admitted her affection for Tennyson to him. There was only one person she'd ever told that much to. He...couldn't know. "Perhaps you should explain these gifts to me again."

He met her gaze. "I've blundered, I can tell... I'm going too fast. No going back now; I must keep moving forward if you're to see the truth." Mathias turned away and stared out at the ocean. "Perhaps we should sit on the blanket for this."

"No," she said vehemently. "I prefer to stand." Anya was too restless to sit still. She wanted answers and much preferred having them as fast as possible. If she sat down, it would be harder to run away if she didn't like what he had to tell her.

"In order to travel through time, a person needs to have certain gifts or travel with someone that has a gift." The muscles in his cheek twitched. "That is an oversimplification. Traveling isn't always that easy, at least not for all of us. As a rule, we don't jump through time unnecessarily. In the case of my ancestor that married the duke in Regency England...that was entirely an accident. Though there were a few instances of time travel on purpose."

"I'm failing to understand why this is important for me to have this information."

He turned toward her and brushed a stray lock of her hair behind her ear. "Because you, my dear, have traveled back in time. Though it was not intentional, or through normal means."

Mathias did know about her coma dream. Did he have visions like he professed Catherine did? Could he read her mind? Was any of that even possible? She hated that he might have invaded her privacy in some way. She refused to admit he was right about any of it though. Anya would not give him that satisfaction. "You are mistaken. I've never left the twentieth century." That was a true statement either way. Even in her dreams she'd still been in the same century.

His lips twitched. "I'm aware," he conceded. "But you did go back a couple decades in the current century."

She cursed in her mind. Anya would not give any indication that he was correct. "How did I manage that while I laid in a coma?"

Anya asked that question for a few reasons: she wanted to know how she did it, how any of it could be possible...and how did he come by the information. It had all felt real to her while she slept. She reasoned it away as nothing but a dream once she opened her eyes in the hospital. It couldn't have been real. None of it made sense to her.

He lifted her hand and rubbed the pad of his thumb over her ring. "This made it possible."

She stared down at the ring her grandmother had given her, the same ring that had been Anastasia's engagement ring. "A ring doesn't allow a person to travel through time." Or take over a person's body…

"Not by itself, no," he conceded. "This allows you to with some limitations." Mathias took a deep breath. "You have a gift, Anya. It's special and rare. It allows you to travel to another time, as long as the object you are focusing on is from the past. It gives you access to that time, through another person."

"That's…it…" Anya's voice trailed off and she had to remind herself to breathe. "You're wrong. It can't be true." Because, if it was, she possessed Anastasia's body and ended up leading her to her death.

"It is," he insisted. "Usually it's only for a short time. It's too hard to hold on to the connection. I can usually only manage several hours, the longest was two days. You were gone for weeks. If not for Vivi recognizing your ring and Catherine's vision, we would not have made the connection."

Anya shook her head several times. She couldn't believe it had been real. She wouldn't. It was all her fault. She'd killed them both by being a stupid wretch. Both Anastasia and Arthur…. She stopped and met his gaze. Those silver blue eyes she'd found familiar before. The ones that reminded her of Arthur. "I think it is time how you explain how you have intimate knowledge about my supposed time travel." Anger replaced the shock and reverberated through her. She suspected she knew the truth, but she wanted to hear him say it aloud.

"Ah," he began. "You're starting to believe me" Mathias's lips tilted upward into a winsome smile. "You recognize him in me, don't you? It's the eyes," he admitted. "It's the only part of us that seems to travel with us. Kind of creepy if you ask me, but no one ever notices except those of us who have the same gift."

"You were Arthur?" she asked, silently willing him to tell her.

"I was," he finally admitted. "Some of the time, not all. You slipped once and told me your real name. I was patient, waiting, and when you did, I knew we would meet again. It took longer than I'd have liked though. For you, it's been no more than days since you returned, for me it has been a couple years."

Anya didn't like it. None of it. She had to get away from him. The betrayal seemed too keen, and it burned through her. They had died. Both of them, and he'd insisted they marry. What had that been about. "Did you know they were going to die?"

"No." He shook his head several times. "I had no way of knowing. They're not important to history, so there's nothing written about them. I truly believed that marriage would protect you, them, us. It could have if they made it back to the embassy."

"What about Anastasia's father?" she asked. "Your family knew him." Knew her...

"He died in the war," he said. "My father lost contact with him, but later learned about his defection to the Nazi cause, and the death of Anastasia. I asked about it after..." He swallowed hard. "It had seemed too real. I needed to understand it, as you do now."

"That's generous of you," she replied bitterly. Anya stared down at the ring on her finger, hating the sight of it. She took it off and threw it at him. "I'm leaving." Somehow, the ring represented something horrible. A time when she believed she could make a difference, and perhaps she had, and a time she might have experienced love. With his admission, that last part didn't seem real. He had taken something precious and ruined it. The memory hurt even more knowing the falsehood behind it. He'd known she wasn't Ana and could have told her at any time. Why hadn't he?

She didn't give him a chance to respond. He'd led her down to the beach so that she had to work to escape, but she would not let that treacherous path prevent her from leaving. It all made sense to her now that she knew the truth. Anya thought she didn't love Arthur, and that was the truth. She hadn't loved him. No, it was much, much worse. She'd fallen in love with Mathias, pretending to be Arthur, and that is why it had been so devastating to see him die. It also explained why Arthur had sometimes been indifferent to her while other times he seemed devoted. It was the worst sort of betrayal. He had known she was someone else and Anya had been in the dark. She needed time to sort out her feelings.

ANYA HAD MADE it back to the manor without incident. Mathias had stayed on the beach. She didn't know why he'd let her go. Perhaps he understood she needed the time away from him. She wandered into the library where he'd taken her the night of her arrival and went over to the mirror. She skimmed her fingers along the edge of it, unable to resist touching it.

"It's beautiful, isn't it?" Lady Vivian said from behind her.

She turned toward her and said, "Yes. What is it about this mirror?" It had called to her before, and it did now. If she stepped into it, would it deliver on its promise? Would it take her away from all her misery and take her someplace different? If it did, would that even help?

"It's allows certain individuals to travel through time," she admitted. "Though I've never experienced it. For us, it's a myth or legend my family has told each generation." She walked over and skimmed the side with her fingertips. "I'm not as gifted as my brother. I can't travel at all. The mirror doesn't speak to me and never will."

"Why not," she asked. It spoke to her. What did that say about her? "Does it not work for anyone with gifts?"

"It is supposed to." Lady Vivian stepped back. "But no one has traveled for generations. The gifts are...weaker, at least in my case. The only one of us that has been able to travel in any fashion is Mathias." She turned to face Anya. "You have the same gift he does. He's been looking for you for some time.

My gifts are...analytical in nature. I remember things is a better way of saying it. He mentioned your name and described the ring one day, and it clicked." Her ring...the one she'd tossed at him? Anya stared at her finger, now bare, and frowned. Had she made another mistake? "After he knew your identity in this time, he started planning. My brother loves you." Lady Vivian tilted her head to the side, and said, "The question is how do you feel about him?"

Anya still had trouble accepting all of it. She had woken up from what she thought to be a dream, only to discover it had all been real. Her feelings for him were complicated. "I don't know."

"Figure it out," she said. "He's a good man. While I don't always agree with his choices, I do know that much. Don't hurt him." With those words, she spun on her heels and left the room.

Lady Vivian had given her a little more to think about. Did she want to give him a chance? Could she really trust him?

She stared at the mirror for several heartbeats uncertain what her next move should be. Should she go look for Mathias? Wait for him to come to her? Would she want a relationship with him that extended beyond their time together in the past? Anya had never been so conflicted in her life.

"I passed my sister in the hall," Mathias said as he entered the room. There was concern in his voice and a little trepidation. Anya couldn't blame him after the way she'd acted previously. She'd be wary too in his place. "She didn't give you too much trouble, did she?"

"No," Anya told him. "She was helping me understand everything a little better." Should she apologize for acting like a spoiled child? He had kept things from her, but maybe he had reasons she'd failed to understand. Sometimes she reacted before actually listening.

"And did she?" He moved closer to her. Her stomach fluttered with nervous energy. She wasn't sure what she wanted from him, but she was ready to stop running. "Help you, that is?"

Anya nodded. "A little." She still had many questions, and it would probably be quite a while before she had a full comprehension of it all.

"Is there anything I can tell you that would alleviate any of your concerns?" He stepped even closer. "What can I do to help you? Name it, and I'll make it happen."

"I don't know that there is any way to make this…work."

He cupped her cheek in his hand. She closed her

eyes as he quoted her favorite verse from "Maud" in a husky tone. It reminded her of that night they discussed poetry.

> "'Half the night I waste in sighs,
> Half in dreams I sorrow after,
> The delight of early skies;
> In a wakeful doze I sorrow,
> For the hand, the lips, the eyes,
> For the meeting of the morrow,
> The delight of happy laughter,
> The delight of low replies.'"

If she tried hard enough, she could picture him in the past with her instead of Arthur; it was him that had actually been there, after all. Her heart beat rapidly inside of her chest. So much uncertainty...

He leaned down and whispered, "I dream of you. Nothing I do can erase that time from my mind. I've missed you and waited. Please don't walk away from me now." Mathias remained completely still. "Would it help if you knew what happened to them...the children."

She jerked at his words. "Oskar and Johanna?" Anya had started to accept that it was all real. Her love was real. This was…real. "You know where they are?"

"They're not children, of course, not anymore, but yes I had them sent to England. They live near Seabrook. Asher made sure they were taken care of." That was Catherine's husband. "It was his contacts that I used to smuggle them out. I asked him, on one of my returns, how to handle it. I know you thought they went to California, but this was for the best. I don't actually have any contacts there, and well, I lied. I'm sorry."

That explained how he'd known what to do. He'd been able to act like quite the spy. "It's enough to know they survived and they're happy." They had done one thing right. At least she could have some comfort in that. Arthur and Ana had died, but the children lived. Not all had been lost… It also told her that Mathias may have made some mistakes, but he meant well. This man also understood her like no one ever had. "I love you," the words were low and her voice hoarse as she spoke. "I'm scared."

"I am too," he admitted. "But I think we can figure it out together." He brushed her hair away from her face. "And I desperately want to kiss you."

"No one is stopping you," she teased.

Mathias didn't need any further encouragement.

He leaned down and pressed his lips to hers. She sighed in contentment. They had a lot to work through, and she had so much to learn about her gift. The last thing she wanted to do was accidently time travel again. That dream, or vision, for lack of a better description, led her to the man she loved with all her heart. That must have been what her grandmother had meant when she'd given it to her. She had told her to follow her heart, and perhaps it was time to follow that advice and give in to what it wanted most—Mathias.

EPILOGUE

Two years later...

Anya stared at the mirror in the library. Something about it still called to her, but she didn't walk over to it. Today was a special day and she had no intention of accidentally time traveling. She was marrying Mathias, and everyone was already outside waiting for her to walk down the aisle.

They had opted for an outdoor wedding that overlooked the cliffs, a simple ceremony that would tie them together legally in ways they already felt emotionally. At the end of it, she'd be his wife, the Marchioness of Blackthorn, but even that didn't matter. The relationship they had built along with their growing love and trust did. She couldn't imagine spending the rest of her life with anyone else.

"You look beautiful," Lady Vivian said. "Now, if you're done primping, I think Mathias might be not-so-patiently waiting for you to meet him at the altar."

"He knows I'll be there," she answered. "He can wait a few more moments." Her heart warmed with joy. There were times she didn't believe she'd ever be this happy or find a way past the pain she'd endured, but with Mathias, she'd found where she belonged. She'd wait for him, and he'd do the same for her. They loved each other, and that was what mattered to her.

Anya glanced at the mirror again. This time to make sure her dress was perfect. It had a high neckline bordered by lace with an A-line skirt that flared out around the hips. The hemline stopped at the knees. She loved how the skirt swished around her when she twirled. The mirror started to swirl a little as she stared into it, and then it cleared a little. It showed another wedding at the estate in the same area where she'd say her vows with Mathias. She didn't recognize the couple, but they didn't matter.

The blonde woman, the Maid of Honor if Anya

had to hazard a guess seemed a little sad. The mirror was trying to tell Anya something about her. After the ceremony, the woman walked along the cliffs, stopped a moment to talk to a white rabbit, then tripped and fell over the edge. Anya gasped. The mirror revealed to her what happened to the woman Mathias told her about. His ancestor that fell and traveled through time.

She smiled. It was a nice wedding present that added validity to her story with Mathias. She hadn't realized she needed it until that moment. Satisfied she was making the best decision for herself, she turned from the mirror and faced Lady Vivian. "I am ready."

They exited the library and met Anya's father in the foyer. Then they walked out to where the ceremony was to be held. Lady Vivian walked down the aisle first, then Anya followed, escorted by her father. The vows went by in a blur, and in the end, it was enough that she could say Mathias was her husband, and she loved him as much as he loved her. Only time would tell if they lived happily ever after, but she certainly hoped they would…

AFTERWORD

Thank you so much for taking the time to read my
book.
Your opinion matters!
Please take a moment to review this book on your
favorite review site and share your opinion with
fellow readers.

www.authordawnbrower.com

TEMPTING AN AMERICAN PRINCESS

MARSDEN DESCENDANTS

CHAPTER ONE

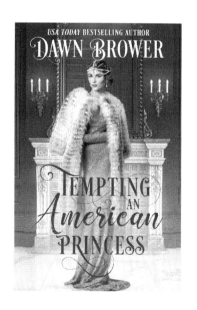

New York, 1911

A train whistle echoed though the tunnel, announcing its arrival at Penn Station. The screech of brakes followed soon after as it slowed to a halt near the exit platform. Brianne Collins stared out the window and took a deep breath. They had arrived, and she couldn't wait to explore everything the city had to offer. Even the train station held something fresh and exciting. Penn Station was shiny and new with pink granite throughout. The station had opened officially six months ago in November. Now that it was spring, her parents had finally agreed to let her come to New York and experience the social life available in the city.

"Do not rush out of the train," her mother, Lilliana Collins, said sternly. She brushed a stray midnight lock behind her ear. "Everyone will be in a hurry, and it will be too easy to lose you in the shuffle. We will exit after most of the occupants already have departed from the platform."

Brianne crinkled her nose in displeasure, but remained seated—even though she fairly itched with anxiety and the urge to move. Trust her mother to take all the fun out of if. Her brother, William, stood and glanced out the window at the platform. "There are a lot of people out there. I don't like it." He ran his hand through his dark hair. His blue eyes, the same shade as their mother's, held a hint of unease in them.

"You don't like anything outside of Lilimar." Their home, renamed after their mother inherited it, was one of the few remaining working plantations in South Carolina. Lilimar was a combination of her mother's name, Lilliana Marsden, before she'd married Brianne's father, Randall Collins. "Please refrain from expounding the virtue of the countryside. We are in New York, and I intend to enjoy it." Brianne flashed William a sanguine smile. "Cheer up dear brother. Once father joins us, you can return to Lilimar and breathe easier."

William would prefer to stay at the plantation and help with running the estate. If their father hadn't been needed in South Carolina, William would have remained at home. The other family business was shipping. It had been combined with Marsden shipping years ago, but their father remained head of the company. It was also half-owned by her uncle Liam Marsden, Viscount Torrington.

A percentage of the shipping company was part of Brianne's dowry. Lilimar was William's inheritance, and he'd own it outright one day. Brianne suspected her mother would sign the deed over to him soon. He did far more on the plantation than anyone else did. "I like spending time with you and mother," William said a little petulantly.

"I'm sure you do, dear," Lilliana told him.

Their father had ordered William to accompany them on the trip to New York. Randall Collins hadn't liked the idea of his wife and daughter traveling to the dangers of the city without a male presence. "You shouldn't placate him, Mother." Brianne rolled her eyes. "It encourages him to act like a petulant child."

William glared at her. "I'm not the child in this train car. I don't understand why you believe you have to go all the way to New York for a season. Couldn't you find someone to marry you in South Carolina?"

Her brother didn't understand. It was about more than finding a suitable man to spend the rest of her days with. She was so...restless. Brianne wanted to do more. Be more. She'd been to England several times visiting family, but sometimes it seemed like she'd led a sheltered life. A man wouldn't provide that missing piece. That had been an excuse to gain her parents' permission to travel to New York. She would be launched into society and meet new people. She craved excitement and purpose. Brianne hoped to find both in the city, and if she didn't, well then, she could travel some place else. "What I require isn't in South Carolina," she answered.

"And you think you'll find it here?" William shook his head, an exasperated expression on his face. "Somehow, I doubt that is your entire purpose. What kind of scheme are you concocting?"

"That's enough," Lilliana Collins ordered. "Gather your belongings; it's time to exit the train." She stood and grabbed her reticule. She didn't say another word as she headed toward the door.

William and Brianne glared at each other for a

few seconds and then followed after her. There were still a lot of people roaming through the train station, but those bustling to exit had diminished some as her mother predicted. She was in awe of the splendor of Penn Station. She'd noted the pink marble earlier, but there were also wide sweeping staircases and stately colonnades. Nothing quite like this structure existed in Charleston. They had some fancy buildings, and the plantation was a thing of beauty to be certain. Lilimar was a home depicting its time with huge pillars, a long sweeping balcony that ran along the whole outside edge and large windows. It even had lush gardens and landscaping to add to the appeal. Lilimar was home, but Brianne couldn't wait to escape it.

She had grown up pampered and privileged, aware of who she was and where she stood in the world. Penn Station made her feel that luxury and also invigorated her. It was full of possibilities and the chance to go places she'd never been. She stared at it all as she moved through the station, not really paying any mind to where she was heading. Brianne bumped into someone and nearly knocked him or her to the ground. "My apologies…" She'd nearly knocked down a lady with dark hair, soft blue eyes, but a severe expression on her face. If Brianne had to guess, she was a few years older than her own nineteen years.

The woman shook her head and frowned. "You should pay more attention."

Brianne had never felt worse. She had been so caught up in everything she hadn't realized where she was going. Not only had she almost knocked this woman to the ground, but she had also managed to separate herself from her mother and brother. "You're right." Brianne nibbled on her lip. "It was foolish of me. Please forgive my blunder."

The woman patted her arm. "We all make mistakes. Think nothing of it." She glanced around. "Are you traveling alone?"

That irritated her a little. It almost sounded as if the other woman was judging her. She seemed to be on her own as well. How was that any concern of hers? "Does it matter?" She lifted a brow.

"No, of course not," the woman answered. "It's a woman's right to do as she pleases. It's why I've been working so hard as an activist in the suffragist movement. But I digress... Let me introduce myself." She held out her hand. "I am Alice Paul."

There was something about that name that tugged on Brianne's memory. She narrowed her gaze and studied her outstretched hand. Slowly, she lifted hers and shook it. Brianne wasn't accustomed to shaking hands. That seemed more of manly thing to do. "Brianne Collins," she offered her name. "To answer your earlier question, I'm not traveling alone. I'm with my mother and brother, but I seem to have been separated from them."

"That's awful. It's such a large city. Do you wish for me to help you locate them?"

It was nice of her to offer, but she didn't want to impose on the woman. It struck her then why her name seemed so familiar. Her cousin Angeline was active in the suffragette movement in England. She was constantly writing to Brianne and telling her about the things she was involved in. Of course, since she married the Marquess of Severn, she'd been doing more behind-the-scenes activities. Lucian didn't like his wife putting herself in danger, but he also wanted her to do something she believed in. Angeline had worked with the Pankhursts, and that was why Alice Paul's name was familiar. Brianne tilted her head to the side and asked, "Are you the same Alice Paul that was jailed in England last year?"

Her cheeks reddened slightly. "Um, yes," she answered. "Admittedly, it wasn't the most splendid of experiences. The force feedings…" She shuddered.

"But the cause is a good one, and I stand by my convictions. Do you follow the suffragette movement in England?"

"Yes and no," Brianne answered. "A family member of mine is active in the cause, but I've not been seeking information myself."

"Oh?" Alice lifted a brow. "Would I know her?"

"Perhaps," Brianne said. "She mentioned you to me a few times in correspondence. Angeline St. John, the Marchioness of Severn."

She frowned. "I do recognize the name, but we didn't have the opportunity to become further acquainted. A pity." She shrugged her shoulders noncommittally. "I have become active in the cause here since my return from England. If you wish to join us…"

"I'm not sure it is something I should do," Brianne interrupted her. She empathized with the cause, but she had no desire to become an active member of their association. Brianne would much rather stay at home than march on the streets or participate in a hunger strike. While she understood their reasoning, she enjoyed the life she had. Why change it? Besides, Alice Paul seemed a bit off-putting, and Brianne wasn't sure she even liked her.

"Every woman should take an active role in their

own lives, don't you think?" She smiled encouragingly. Several people pushed past them, and they really should move or end their conversation. Penn Station was crowded and their impromptu conversation had to be irritating some people. "Do you not have opinions of your own and exercise them whenever you can? There has to be times you wish that you could do as you please and not have to ask permission. Think about it, and if you choose to join the movement, send me a missive. I'm in the city for a few days, and then I'm returning home." Brianne glanced around, hoping to find one of her family members. She desperately needed a reason to abandon this conversation.

"I'll keep that in mind." She really didn't want to become embroiled in the suffragist movement. Brianne rather liked her life as it was. Why should she change anything about it? Something caught her attention, and she glanced past Alice Paul. She emitted a sigh of relief. Her mother and brother were on the far side of the room. "If you'll excuse me, I noticed my family over there, and I should join them. It was nice making your acquaintance."

"It was a pleasure, even if you did almost knock me over. I hope to hear from you again." With those words, Alice Paul left Brianne alone.

She turned to walk to her mother and brother and ran into a hard, male chest. *Drat*. Wasn't that her luck? First Alice Paul, and now this unsuspecting gentleman... "Pardon me," she said.

"Do you know the woman you were conversing with?" the man asked. He had a rich English accent that reminded her of her grandfather Thor. It held a hint of authority to it. His hair was as dark as the night sky, and his eyes the color of the sky during a storm—a mix of gray and blue.

"I cannot fathom why that would be any of your concern," she answered. "As I'm most definitely not acquainted with you." Brianne glanced up at the man and held in a breath. He was gorgeous. If she were to be honest with herself, she had to admit he was the handsomest male she'd ever had the pleasure of gazing upon. If he wasn't being rude she might consider flirting with him.

His lips twitched slightly. "I suppose you're correct."

"There is no supposition involved. We've never been introduced."

"I'm not disagreeing with you," he replied cajolingly. "However, I am acquainted with your family. I have seen you even though we've never been introduced."

That took her aback. "I don't believe you."

He chuckled softly and turned slightly so she could see her brother and mother heading in their direction. "Is that not your family there?" He lifted a brow. "I'm acquainted with William. Andrew and Alexander I am familiar with. They are dear friends of mine. Went to Eton and then Oxford with them."

Of course he had... What were the chances? "As you have me at a disadvantage, why don't you introduce yourself."

"Lord Julian Kendall," he said and bowed. "Now, about that woman..."

"She's no concern of yours," Brianne interrupted him. She didn't need any lectures. Especially as she had no intention of becoming involved with the likes of Alice Paul.

"But you *do* know who she is?"

"Of course I do," she answered. "But I don't need to explain myself to you. You're not my brother or my father. We're barely acquainted. Now, if you'll excuse me, I must join my family."

She didn't allow him to say another word. Brianne brushed past him and went toward her mother and brother. They had finally noticed her, and William stepped in her direction. Brianne nodded at him and motioned for him to stay in place. It would be easier if they weren't both moving. She had no desire to be separated from them again. Two unwanted conversations hadn't been pleasant for her, and she'd had more than enough of Penn Station. In fact, she was starting to dislike it. So far, it hadn't led her anywhere good.

*J*ulian Kendall strolled to Hotel Irving, located at 26 Gramercy Park South. It was an exclusive hotel located on the Island of Manhattan. Nothing about New York or America appealed to him.

Julian finally reached the hotel and walked inside. A clerk greeted him immediately. "Hello, sir," a man with dark brown hair and gray on the sides near his ear stated. "How may I assist you?"

"My name is Lord Julian Kendall. Did you receive a telegram about a reservation for me?"

The man leaned down and scanned the contents of a ledger and then nodded. "Your telegram said you would be here for an indefinite amount of time."

"Indeed," Julian replied. "I hope to make New

York my home away from home." He flashed him one of his most charming smiles. "What I've seen so far has made me think I'll be here for quite a while." Not a lie. Bumping into Brianne Collins had been quite serendipitous.

The clerk turned around and opened a cabinet, then snatched a set of keys off of a hook. He dangled them before Julian. "The curved one is for your room, and the one with a G emblazoned upon it is for the gate at Gramercy Park. Feel free to take advantage of the park, but it is exclusive. Only those with a key can use it. Please don't let any riffraff into the park. There are ladies that use it regularly, and we want to ensure their safety."

What a novel idea... None of the parks in London were gated quite like this. They were trying to keep unsavory individuals out of the park and make its use solely for the higher class. What were the chances someone on the poorer side would venture over to this part of Manhattan? Seemed like the rich class swarmed this area. He hadn't noticed anyone else. Not even a member of the working class... Did they have a rule about allowing them out in public or something?

"Thank you," Julian said as politely as possible. He'd grown up privileged, but he'd never been slapped in the face with it before, or perhaps he hadn't noticed before. "Can you direct me to my room?"

"Go up the stairs and make a right. The room is all the way on the end on the left-hand side."

"My trunks will be sent over from Penn Station. Please have them brought to my room when they arrive." He'd hired someone to see to his baggage when he'd arrived. All he'd brought with him on his trek over to the hotel was a small valise. He clutched the keys in one hand and his bag in the other, then went in the direction the clerk indicated. It didn't take him long to arrive at his room. He slid the key into the lock and turned it. Once the lock clicked open, he pushed the door open and entered.

It was a luxurious room. A matching chair and side table was near the window. A fireplace was on the opposite side of the room from small settee, and a table had been placed near it. In a separate, smaller room, a plush bed with a dark maroon coverlet and gold embroidery filled the area. There was another small table on the side of the bed. Light illuminated the bedroom area from two French style doors that led out to a balcony.

It wasn't as large as his rooms in London, but they'd do. The hotel did an excellent job of appealing to the finer tastes of the rich and entitled. He should fit in, and somehow, that left a bitter taste in his mouth. Julian set his bag on the bed and went over to the washbasin located at the opposite side of the room. Water had already been put in the pitcher. He poured some into the matching bowl and splashed water on his face and dried it with a nearby towel. It refreshed him and washed away some of the grime from travel. Perhaps he'd check out this Gramercy Park...

He pocketed the keys and exited his room, suddenly restless. He could walk around the area and maybe find a gentleman's club. He could use a drink or several. Sleep would prove elusive in the meantime. Julian exited the hotel and whistled as he made his way down the street. The park was pretty close, but he didn't really want to explore it at the moment.

"Julian," a male shouted.

He stopped in his tracks. No one should know he'd arrived or was even in New York. Slowly, he turned toward the sound and relief flooded him. Of course William Collins would seek him out. He'd seen him talking to Brianne at Penn Station. He pasted a happy grin on his face and greeted the other man. "Are you staying around here?" He didn't know what else to say to him.

William bobbed his head up and down. "Yes, father bought a townhouse around the corner. It's the place to be in Manhattan right now. He liked the idea of a locked park for mother and Brianne to take a stroll in."

That would be a nice side benefit to Gramercy Park. If his sister or mother were here, he'd feel better knowing they should be safe in an exclusive park. "I'm staying at the Irving Hotel," Julian gestured toward the place he'd left. "How long are you in town? Isn't it a busy time at the plantation?" He knew next to nothing about what work would be needed at Lilimar. It seemed like a reasonable question to ask.

"I'd rather not be here at all," William replied. He glared at her mulishly. "But someone had to accompany my mother and sister. Father will be here in a couple weeks, and then I'll return home. There's always something that needs to be done at Lilimar." He tilted his head to the side. "What brings you here? Bored with England?"

In some ways, he was, and that gave him the perfect excuse to explore what America had to offer.

"I've been everywhere else with my tour and all that. Father thought it would be good for me to see how things worked in America." Julian shrugged. "I doubt I'll do anything that will add growth to my character." His father was unaware of his tendency to work as a spy, and Julian intended to keep it that way. Acting like a rogue of sorts worked fine for the persona he wanted to display for the world. "Do you happen to know of a good gentleman's club around here?"

"The Player's Club is around the corner at 16 Gramercy South," William replied. "It's a members-only club."

Julian narrowed his gaze and asked, "Does that mean I can't gain admittance?" It sounded like exactly the place he needed entrance to. The who's who of the New York elite would probably have membership.

William smiled. "Not exactly." He gestured toward the pathway that would lead toward the club. "I happen to be a member. Follow me, and I'll nominate you for admittance. Though, I should warn you, it has a pricey fee to join, but well worth it if you want any privacy. I'm in New York far more than I'd like, and joining the club was a necessity." He sighed. "I was heading there when I noticed you in front of me. My sister tries my patience. I had to escape for a little while."

That seemed like an opening to discuss Brianne's proclivities. Instead he took a slightly different approach. "I understand. My own sister is difficult on a good day." He pushed his hands into his pockets as they walked. "I had a small encounter with yours at Penn Station. She wasn't inclined to accept my assistance."

William rolled his eyes and said in a disgusted tone, "She believes she knows what is best about everything and won't listen to reason. If she got her head out of the clouds long enough to actually see the world around her, she might not have been separated from us after we exited the train. It was pure luck that we found her relatively fast."

Not fast enough if she had time for a tête-à-tête with Alice Paul… He'd wait to broach that topic of conversation with William at a later date. For now, he'd gain entrance to this club of his and explore it. "Tell me about the Player's Club," Julian encouraged him.

"It was founded in 1888 by Edwin Booth," William began. "He wanted to use the club as a way to wipe away the tarnish on the Booth name. His younger brother was John Wilkes Booth."

"Ah," Julian replied. "Assassination of a president would make one's name less than desirable..."

"I wouldn't have wanted to be him. If I had a brother, and he'd done something so profoundly stupid, and he hadn't been tracked down by Union soldiers and shot—I might have had to do the deed myself."

"Luckily you won't have to find out. No one can possibly be that stupid again." Julian chuckled lightly. He would never attempt an assassination of that multitude himself, but he could see why someone upset with the person in charge might be foolish enough to at least try. "Though your sister might prove to be the bane of your existence."

"Too true," William agreed. "I love her, but she's quite the termagant."

They rounded the corner and headed up to the Player's Club. William pulled open the door and gestured for them to go inside. The main room had a large marble fireplace with a burgundy settee as the focal point in front of it. Two matching chairs flanked it. A nearby staircase was embellished with a plush red carpet. What Julian presumed to be a dining area was to the left beyond the staircase. A long table with at least twenty chairs surrounded it. Several pieces of fine art hung on the walls. "This is quite the lavish place…" He gestured to a painting. "Isn't that a…" He pointed to a painting of bright pink and white flowers in a white vase. It could have been a Van Gogh or a Monet, but Julian wasn't certain.

William shrugged. "I don't know much about art. Though Mark Twain used to be a regular member here. I think one of his original manuscripts is on display. I haven't had a chance to browse many of the items they keep here."

Interesting… "Is this a club for artists?"

"It is mostly," William confirmed. "There are others that aren't exactly artists, but they do create things."

He wasn't sure what that meant. "Explain please."

"Nikola Tesla is a member," William offered.

Julian wasn't that familiar with the physicist's work, but he had heard the name before. A scientist wasn't an artist, but they did indeed explore the possibilities of the world. "Do I need to have some sort of gift in order to become a member."

"I don't," William said. "They like to keep a mix of artists, for lack of a better word, and the upper class. It's the Player's Club's way of keeping channels open for struggling individuals and keeping their genius going."

This Player's Club would be far more interesting than he'd originally thought... "In that case..." He gestured toward William. "Take me to the person I need to discuss a membership with."

It didn't' take long to convince the patrons to consider his membership. They couldn't admit him on the spot. It would have to go up for a vote, but the main members didn't think it would be a problem. They liked the addition of including the son of a duke in their books. Julian liked the information pool he'd be able to dip into. It was far better than he could have hoped for. If the rest of his visit to New York went as well, he might be able to return home sooner than he'd hoped, and maybe get a better assignment in the process.

This assignment of his hadn't been one he'd wanted to accept, but he'd felt he had to. If he wanted to make a name for himself, he had to take the necessary steps to show the higher ups they could depend on him—no matter how distasteful the duty might be. He'd been sent over to New York because they wanted someone there to observe the efforts of the suffragists.

England had its own issues regarding women's rights, and it was prudent that they understood the climate everywhere. Alice Paul was an American who had become embroiled with the Pankhursts in England, and it had been her that caught the attention of government officials. Part of his assignment was to ensure she didn't return. Her last stint in the jail system hadn't been—pleasant. Of course, that was a mild term for what she'd endured. By her own stubbornness for her cause, she could have died of starvation, and they'd been forced to feed her against her will. Luckily, she'd survived and then returned home. As long as she stayed where she belonged, she shouldn't be a problem for England again.

Even though Alice Paul was part of his assignment, she wasn't the entirety of it. He wouldn't be following her around and spying on her. It would look strange if he did. He was a member of the aristocracy, and it would be easier for him to infiltrate New York society. He'd do his part to appear like a gentleman of means, and in his spare time, he'd poke around the suffragist movement. There were probably females in the upper classes dissatisfied with the status quo too. Miss Brianne Collins appeared to be one of them...

Her relations to his friends Alexander and Andrew Marsden made it easier for him to become closer to her. It had also given him a reason to speak to her at Penn Station, but that didn't mean she trusted him. Miss Collins had seemed to think he was distasteful to glance upon. He'd have to make an effort to change her mind. She could be the one person he needed to spy on the suffragists and report their progress back home. The men in high society were his other targets. They were the ones who would control the climate in the States and at a higher level in the federal government. Since they held all the cards, so to speak, it would ultimately be up to them if a change were made.

In some ways, Julian wasn't sure why they cared about what was going on in America. Why couldn't England decide on its own whether or not to grant women more rights without knowing what was happening around the world. It was a tough issue and he could see why men didn't want to relinquish the control they'd had for well—ever; however, women should have the ability to choose for themselves what they wanted for their lives without anyone dictating to them. That didn't mean he condoned some of the practices the Pankhursts took part in. They were dangerous and radical.

Nevertheless, he'd do his duty. Whether he liked it or not.

EXCERPT: CHARMING HER ROGUE

LINKED ACROSS TIME

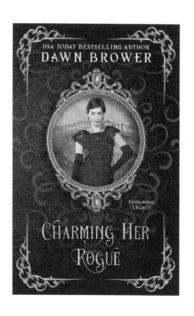

CHAPTER ONE

June 18, 1914

ady Catherine Langdon twirled the champagne in her glass, staring at the bubbles as they popped against the side of the crystal. Music echoed throughout the room as a violinist strummed out Vivaldi's *The Four Seasons*. Catherine would have preferred something a little more soothing to ease her current distress, but she didn't have much say for anything in her life. She considered herself a modern woman, yet she had to continue to follow the dictates of society.

At one and twenty, she'd have liked to have found her own residence and used her inheritance as she saw fit. That wasn't to be her fate though. Her father had ensured she had a guardian for all things, and she wouldn't have control of her funds for four more years. If she married, they'd go to her husband. Catherine didn't have any intention of allowing something so archaic to happen to her. No man would ever have power over her.

"Do you find these dinners dreary too?" a male asked from behind her.

She'd been so caught up in her own thoughts that she'd failed to notice his presence until he'd spoken. Catherine turned to glance up at him. He was tall and foreboding. Some ladies might be intimidated by that, but not Catherine. He had golden blond hair with highlights streaked throughout that suggested he spent time outdoors in full sunlight. One strand fell loose over his forehead in an enticing curl. His eyes were like shiny emeralds that mesmerized her for a few brief moments until she regained her composure.

"They can be rather tedious," she confirmed. "But they appear to be a necessity for the ambassador." Sir Benjamin Villiers, her guardian, worked as secretary to the ambassador. Catherine had been living in France with him since her father's death over a year ago. Some ladies would have been excited to live in Paris and have access to the latest fashions, but not her—never her. Catherine's dark hair came from her father, the former Duke of Thornly, but her sapphire blue eyes were from her mother. Her father's title had passed on to a cousin she'd been barely acquainted with. Her mother had died in childbirth —after one of the several times she tried to give the duke an heir he desperately needed—or more apt— wanted. Unfortunately, neither her mother nor the child survived. She was completely alone in the world, and sometimes that was more than she could bear.

She wanted so much more than pretty gowns and shiny baubles. They were nice, and she did appreciate not having to worry about money. Some things were far more important though. She'd been secretly studying to become a nurse. Sir Benjamin would be appalled if he found out. She prayed he continued to remain ignorant of her pastime. With the current climate of the political world, she feared such skills might prove necessary—though she prayed her instincts proved wrong.

Certain gifts had been bestowed upon members of her family that dated back centuries. Some of her ancestors had been persecuted as witches. Her mother was a direct descendant of that line, and now her. Catherine's name came from a variation of one of those long-ago witches—Caitrìona. Catherine even had the same gift as the woman who'd been presumed wicked and a servant of the devil. Those who didn't understand their abilities chose to believe the people who had them were immoral, but her family considered their abilities a blessing from someplace good.

The thing about gifts—sometimes they came in threes. She'd been somehow blessed with all of the abilities, but one remained stronger than the rest. Her premonitions didn't come in flashes, but more like feelings emphasized by the emotions of people around her. Her strongest and most reliable ability centered around that amplification, and sometimes she had trouble deciphering what it all meant. This man projected one thing loudly —secrets. He was hiding something, and whatever it turned out to be could potentially impact the world.

"Some people need society events to function," he said evenly. "I've never been one to put stock in them. Do you enjoy them?"

"Not particularly," she replied. "As you've stated —they're more tiresome than entertaining. If you don't like them, what brings you to this particular one? The ambassador's guests are generally of the prestigious sort."

She'd met numerous individuals that boasted of their importance. Catherine hadn't found any of them especially noteworthy. She hadn't relied on her gifts for any epiphanies where they were concerned. In her experience, if someone talked that much about themselves, it usually meant they were of little consequence. It was the quiet ones she had to watch and figure out. Like this man—he'd started the conversation, but gave little of himself away.

"It's not my practice to boast about my connections." He reached out and snatched a glass of champagne from a waiter as he strolled past. The man brought it to his lips and sipped the bubbly liquid. Once again, Catherine was transfixed by him, his deeds, and his inaction. Everything about him remained an enigma. What game was he playing? He lowered his glass and met her gaze. "Don't you think it is far better to blend in and not allow anyone to notice you?"

She didn't understand how he'd ever be able to make himself unnoticeable. He was by far the most handsome man in the room, and he oozed charm and arrogance, but perhaps he only showed her that side of himself. He seemed to be a man made up of several facets. He had his charm, the easy-going nature he showed the world, but his eyes had a darkness to them that suggested he had something to hide. But she didn't need to rely completely on suppositions. She'd been born with the ability to see past the façades people used to hide who they truly were. This man had an aura that screamed of secrecy. "I've never been much of a wallflower," she replied. "I enjoy social interaction—most of the time." In fact, she almost needed it.

He tilted his head. "No, you wouldn't be. A woman like you stands out in a crowd. You must have numerous suitors."

"Not particularly," she answered. "At least not here in France. Back home I had a few." None of them made her heart beat faster or her breathing shallow. This man did though. Something about him made her want to move closer, to touch him, and maybe even press her lips to his. To make it simple, he was dangerous to her well-being, and she still didn't even know his name.

"That's a bloody shame." He sipped his sparkling wine again. "I expect you'd be like this champagne. Sweet, tantalizing, and overflowing with pleasure after one taste."

He had to be a rogue of the worst sort. Gentleman didn't say such outrageous things to a lady. Did he believe her to be a cyprian hired for the enjoyment of the men at the party? There were not many females in attendance. Such was the nature of political work—women stayed home more often than not. The other ladies there were wives of the diplomats and their employers. Catherine was the sole unattached woman in attendance. Perhaps she was reading too much into his statement.

"Sir, you're too bold." She narrowed her eyes to glare at him. "I insist you apologize."

He lifted a brow. "You're not any of those things I mentioned?" His lips tilted upward into a sinful smile. Damn him and his gorgeous face. "I don't believe it."

"I'm not a lady you can insult without consequences." She was the daughter of a duke, damn it. Catherine lifted her chin and pinned him with her most haughty stare. "Do you not know who I am?"

He chuckled lightly. "I think all of France is aware of your lineage—certainly everyone in England is."

Catherine took a deep breath and prepared for the impending disagreement. This man rubbed her wrong—and right, at the same time. She fervently wished she didn't find him so attractive. Her body almost hummed with joy in his presence. She'd always followed her instincts in the past; however, she believed, with him, she'd best exercise caution. He was able to hide a part of himself from her gifts, and she couldn't trust him because of that. What made him special?

"Then why do you persist in being so discourteous?" For the life of her, she couldn't discern his motivation for being so arrogant and condescending. She was pleasant to everyone, and he made her want to punch someone for the first time in her entire life. "What have I done for you to be this way with me?"

"Not a thing." He shrugged. "You intrigue me, and I thought I'd ascertain your mettle."

"Ohh..." If she was a lady inclined to give into temper tantrums, she'd already be stomping her foot and screaming at the top of her lungs. "You're insufferable."

"Thank you." His lips twitched, and amusement fairly danced out of his eyes. "I do pride myself in being able to needle people in the most unexpected ways."

She rolled her eyes. "In that case, consider your goal achieved."

Catherine disliked him. He was the worst sort of man, and she couldn't fathom what she'd found so compelling before. He could go back to hell as far as she was concerned. It would be a happy day if she never came in contact with him ever again. Some handsome devils shouldn't be encouraged, and he was at the top of that list.

"Does one dance at these things?" He glanced around the room. "It seems as if most people are content with talking about inane topics sure to put me to sleep."

"Let me guess," she began. "You consider yourself and everything about you the very epitome of all that is exhilarating in the world." God save her from men who thought the world revolved around them. She didn't need their ilk paying any attention to her.

"Not at all," he replied smoothly. "But I'm not so boring as to engender individuals into a catatonic state." He gestured to a nearby group. "Just look at them all—their very faces allude to placidity— they're practically asleep standing up."

Catherine sighed. "If you're in such a state of ennui why are you still here?" For that matter, why did she continue to converse with him? She was well past the stage of irritation and had entered into complete annoyance. "You could go home, and all would be well in your world, Mr.—"

"Lord," he interrupted her. "I've never been a mere mister."

Of course he was a *lord*. Arrogance such as his came naturally to some, but those of his ilk were weaned on it. No wonder he oozed it as easily as breathing and didn't apologize for it. "Be that as it may…" She silently prayed for patience. "To answer your earlier question, this was never meant to be the dancing sort of gathering. It's a dinner and conversation. If you want more, you should attend the ball later this week. I'm sure a lord such as yourself will have no problem finding a willing dance partner."

"Will you dance with me?" His lips tilted upward into a sinful smile. His arrogance and self-assurance flowed through her in waves. "That is why you suggested I attend the next ball is it not?" He lifted a brow questioningly.

The polite thing would be to say yes. That was what was expected of her, after all… "Absolutely not." She couldn't stop herself from saying it. "I don't believe we'd manage a full set before I wanted to strangle you. It's best to save us both from that disastrous outcome."

Instead of being offended, he grinned widely as if she'd complimented him. He was such a contrary bastard. "I think I like you."

"Please don't," she begged. "I don't need you to be charming. Liking you is the last thing I wish to do."

At the start of their conversation she'd have liked nothing more. Now that she'd spent some time in his company she'd had a change of heart. He might be handsome, and something about him may call out to her, but he was entirely wrong for her. In her experience, it was better to cut all ties in situations such as this one. Catherine didn't need any heartache in her life.

"Ah," He leaned in a little closer. Heat flowed from him to her in waves. "But you do find me fascinating. If it helps, I'm equally charmed by you."

"I assure you that was not my intention." Her cheeks flushed as she warmed from the inside out. She sipped her champagne absentmindedly for lack of any other response to his attention. "Don't take it to heart."

"I fear I already have." He lifted his champagne glass in salute. "But I know when to take a bow. To you, my dear, Lady Catherine." He took a sip after his toast and then winked. "Until we meet again, for I'm sure we will."

With those words, he exited the room. No one noticed, and she wondered briefly if she'd imagined him. No, her premonitions didn't work that way. He'd been real and present. She couldn't help but believe his parting words an omen of sorts—she wished he'd have at least introduced himself. A name would have been nice to know... Catherine fully expected they would cross paths more than once. Somehow, some way, their lives were intertwined. She'd never been wrong before; nonetheless, this was the first time it both terrified and invigorated her all at once.

CHAPTER TWO

*T*he flat that Asher Rossington, the Earl of Carrick, had secured for his time in Paris had little to offer. His home in England had a more lavish style to it—but nothing less could be expected from Seabrook. His father—the current Marquess of Seabrook—had thought he needed to explore the world a bit. With limited funds at his disposal, Asher didn't see the point in letting something fancier. All he needed was someplace to sleep in relative peace and comfort.

What his father didn't know was that Asher had been actively engaging in a secret mission with the Earl of Derby—who worked closely with the Under-Secretary of State for War. For whatever reason, the old goat didn't trust his cousin, Sir Benjamin Villiers

—who was currently employed by the Ambassador of the United Kingdom to France. The position gave Sir Benjamin access to a variety of foreign officials. Asher didn't know what he'd done to make his cousin distrust him so, but he didn't see any reason why he couldn't do a little spy work while he was off finding himself. It did run in the family, after all. His great-grandfather—Dominic Rossington, the tenth Marquess of Seabrook, had been a spy during the Napoleonic Wars. He liked the idea of following in his footsteps.

A knock echoed through the room. Asher stared at the door as if it were a foreign substance. Who the hell could possibly be on the other side of it? Sure, opening it would give him the answer to that question, but he had no desire to take the effort. If he ignored it long enough, they'd go away and he could be left in peace. The person knocked again. Asher sighed, then stood and walked over to it. Once he reached it, he yanked it open.

"Telegram monsieur," a boy said and shoved an envelope at him, then left.

The front of the envelope was addressed to the Marquess of Seabrook. "Wait, this isn't for me." It couldn't be for him. His father was the marquess. He wouldn't hold that title until... Asher swallowed hard. The only way he'd inherit it was if his father died.

"I deliver them," the boy stopped momentarily and said over his shoulder, "It is up to you what you do with it"

He kept going, not once looking back. Did he not grasp what his delivery meant? His whole life had been turned upside down by one envelope, and he hadn't even broken the seal yet. His father wasn't in France. He should be home at Seabrook—safe and alive. Asher swallowed hard and slowly broke open the envelope. He pulled the missive out, and then fell to his knees. His father… God, he couldn't even think about it. Why had he insisted on Asher having a bloody world tour? The words blurred before him, and he realized why. Tears flowed—he wiped them away furiously, but it didn't help.

He was now the Marquess of Seabrook.

The telegram said his father had died months ago, but they didn't know where to find Asher. So he hadn't even been able to attend his father's funeral. He'd been in Paris for three weeks; before that, he'd been on a boat sailing around Greece, and then he'd taken a train through most of Europe until he decided to work with the Earl of Derby. He'd run into him by chance while in the south of France.

Now he was in Paris, facing the fact his father died while he had gallivanted through multiple countries.

He should go home—even if the funeral had been held already. His mother would need his support, and his sisters... They would all be devastated too. Asher couldn't believe his father was gone... Somehow, he managed to crawl back to his feet and set the telegram on a nearby table. At some point, he'd want to re-read it. He should get out of his flat and walk around Paris. Maybe he'd be able to gather his thoughts and make a decision. There was still work he had to do in the city regarding Sir Benjamin. He couldn't say a final goodbye to his father, and going back to England now seemed almost—pointless. Still, he wouldn't make that decision yet.

Asher headed over to the sink to wash away the tears. His insides were torn to shreds, and his emotions jumped all over the place. It would be a while before he could make any rational decisions, and even longer before his grief ebbed. He grabbed a cloth off the shelf and soaked it in warm water, then scrubbed his face—probably longer than necessary, but it soothed him. He wrung it out and set it on the back of the sink, then stared at his reflection in the overhead mirror. His eyes were rimmed red, and his blond hair remained a little damp from the cloth.

Hopefully no one noticed how wretched he looked. Hell, he didn't really care if they did, as long as they didn't bother asking what was wrong with him. That one question he didn't want to answer. Partially because he didn't have a clue how.

"Well," he said to himself. "At least I'm not a duke—that would be worse. All those 'Your Graces' would drive me mad." He might be a higher rank, but he was still a lord. Some people might take more notice of him though. A marquess had more pull in the government and society. His father had been a major influence in the House of Lords. That was something Asher would have to consider too. How much did he want to participate in politics?

He walked over and grabbed his jacket. The fresh air would do him good, and it wasn't too hot for June yet. Maybe he'd do the tourist thing. He hadn't had time since he arrived. Truthfully, he was looking for anything to think about other than the news shattering his world. He prayed a distraction of some sort would find its way to him.

LADY CATHERINE STROLLED along the side of the *Pont d'Iéna,* heading toward the Eiffel Tower. She had sneaked out of the embassy to explore the area on her own. Sir Benjamin would have insisted she take someone with her. He believed Paris to be an unsafe place for a young lady. Catherine wanted a little peace and quiet. Strolling along the Seine had seemed like a good idea. Something about the water soothed her soul. She stopped and stared at the river below.

"Don't tell me you're considering something drastic," a male said.

She shook herself out of her reverie and glanced up into *his* green eyes. It had been two days since she'd met him at the embassy. He'd been on her mind ever since. Something she wished she didn't have to admit to—even if it was only to herself. Catherine still didn't know his name, and it irritated her that he hadn't introduced himself. Asking her guardian would have solved the problem; however, it would have caused a new one.

Sir Benjamin would have liked that she'd taken an interest in another male. He did want her to marry and settle down, and something told her he'd have loved it even more when he discovered who she'd been interested in. She might not know his name, but she was certain he had a nice title to go with it. Catherine glared at him. "Depends on what you consider drastic."

"Jumping to your death in the river below."

She stared down at the water and shrugged. "Doesn't seem so bad down there. The jump isn't that high—it's survivable."

He lifted a brow. "You *were* contemplating it."

Taking a swim in the Seine was not high on her list of things to do. There were far better things she could do with her time. She wouldn't explain that to him though. They were barely acquainted, and she owed him nothing. "If I did, would you jump in after me?"

"As a gentleman, I'd be required to," he said almost regrettably. "Please don't make me. I've already had a rather bad day, and I'd be grateful if you didn't make it worse."

"I might consider taking pity on you," she teased. "For a price." She started to smile, but when she glanced at him, sadness crashed through her. The empathy side of her gift didn't usually come out so harshly. He grieved, and hard... He hadn't been lying when he said he'd had a bad day. What had caused him so much pain?

"Name it," he answered. "I might be willing to pay

it." He lifted his lips upward, but there was no happiness there. His eyes even showed a little red around them as if he'd cried. This man had actually shed tears—Catherine couldn't hold the surprise in. Her mouth fell open, yet no words came out. "Cat got your tongue?" The following smirk made her want to wipe it off his face. She'd been feeling sorry for him…

"No," she replied. "Debating what I want."

"A lady such as yourself is bound to be pricy." He winked. "I promise I'm good for it."

He made it sound so suggestive. Catherine's cheeks burned, but she couldn't look away. When she'd left the embassy she never expected her day would involve him. The mystery man whom she wanted to learn more about—the enigma she couldn't solve. "Perhaps there is something you can do for me."

"Oh?" He folded his arms over his chest. "I thought that was the point of this conversation. I'm to pay whatever price you deem acceptable so you don't plunge to your death in the river below." He glanced over the railing. "Please tell me you've reconsidered. I don't wish to get wet today."

She rolled her eyes. "You need not worry. I have no desire to die at the moment." Catherine held out her arm to him. "Will you walk with me?"

He tried to hide it, but the grief hadn't gone away. Every second she spent in his company, that sorrow beat into her. She had to help him, or it would grow. "If you insist," he agreed. "I don't particularly want to return to my flat."

Catherine looped her arm through his. "I hear the Eiffel Tower is nice."

"I wouldn't know," he said. "Never been there."

"It's hard to miss." Catherine laughed lightly and pointed toward it. "It's rather large."

He was quiet and didn't acknowledge what she'd gestured to. Catherine wasn't sure how much more she could take. She had to find a way for him to open up. They would be near the tower soon, and then what? "Are you ever going to introduce yourself to me?"

That made him frown even more. What had she said? Why was his name making him ever sadder than before? They reached the end of the bridge, and he pulled away from her. He turned toward the river and stared at it. "Maybe it was me who wanted to jump and you're the one who saved me."

"It can't be that bad." She reached up and touched his arm. "What is wrong?"

"Life is funny," he began. "You think that you have so much time, but really it's quite finite. Any day could be our last, and yet we continue moving forward."

He'd lost someone. That was why he permeated sorrow. "That's also what makes life beautiful. When you find joy, it should be embraced, and even the hard times teach us something. It gives us a reason to appreciate happiness when we do have it."

Their close proximity made it easier for her to reach into him. This side of her gift didn't always work when she wanted it to. If it did, she might be able to alleviate some of his suffering and make the grief easier to bear. A touch of happiness and a sprinkle of hope—then his outlook would improve. He blinked several times and shook his head. "Did you feel that?"

"What?" Catherine asked innocently. Normally people didn't notice when she helped them with her empathic ability. Maybe she had a bigger connection to this man than she realized. She wasn't sure what it meant, but she'd ponder over all the possibilities later—when she was alone.

"That jolt..." He crinkled his eyebrows together. "You really didn't feel it?"

Catherine could never admit that she'd used anything out of the ordinary to heal him. No one understood her gifts. Her family had been cursed enough by them over the years, and she didn't want him to see her differently. For some reason, she liked him. "I'm afraid I don't know what you're talking about."

He shook his head again. "I suppose it's nothing." His lips tilted upward into a sinful smile. The kind he'd first bestowed upon her at the embassy. He already seemed to be more himself. "You asked if I'd ever introduce myself. Would it be too much for you to call me Ash? I don't like formalities."

"If you insist—Ash," she answered. Why didn't he want her to know who he was? What could he possibly be hiding? He admitted he was a lord already. Since he was aware of her familial relations, surely he must realize that she didn't care about his status amongst the ton. "Then you must call me Cat. All my friends do." Not that she had many, but he didn't need to know that.

"I'm rather glad I ran into you." Ash brushed a stray lock of her hair behind her ear. "I think I needed to find my own Kitty-Cat to make me feel better. Thank you for whatever you did."

"I didn't..." The last thing she'd expected when suggesting he use her nickname was that he'd create one of his own. Catherine wasn't sure how she felt about it either. No one had ever bothered to get that familiar with her before. A part of her liked it, the other part of her was terrified by what it could mean.

"I don't need to know," he interrupted. "Just understand it's appreciated. Now come with me. I know a little café that has amazing coffee, and I'd like to spend the afternoon with you."

Catherine didn't push, and neither did he. She let him lead her to the café and the afternoon of laughter that followed. Maybe she'd needed Ash as much as he'd needed her. Fate had a funny way of stepping in that way.

ABOUT THE AUTHOR

USA TODAY Bestselling author, DAWN BROWER writes both historical and contemporary romance. There are always stories inside her head; she just never thought she could make them come to life. That creativity has finally found an outlet.

Growing up she was the only girl out of six children. She is a single mother of two teenage boys; there is never a dull moment in her life. Reading books is her favorite hobby and she loves all genres.

BB bookbub.com/authors/dawn-brower
f facebook.com/AuthorDawnBrower
twitter.com/1DawnBrower
instagram.com/1DawnBrower
g goodreads.com/dawnbrower

Broken Pearl

Deadly Benevolence

A Wallflower's Christmas Kiss

A Gypsy's Christmas Kiss

Snowflake Kisses

Diamonds Don't Cry

Kindred Lies

Begin Again

There You'll Be

Better as a Memory

Won't Let Go

Enduring Legacy

The Legacy's Origin

Charming Her Rogue

Scandal Meets Love

Love Only Me (Amanda Mariel)

Find Me Love (Dawn Brower)

Bluestockings Defying Rogues

Marsden Descendants

Scheming with My Duke

Secluded with My Hellion

Secrets of My Beloved

Spying on My Scoundrel

Shocked by My Vixen

Will My Rogue Love Me Tomorrow

Heart's Intent

One Heart to Give

Unveiled Hearts

Heart of the Moment

Kiss My Heart Goodbye

Heart in Waiting

Coming Soon

A Heart Redeemed

Heart Lessons

Broken Curses

The Enchanted Princess

The Bespelled Knight

The Magical Hunt

Ever Beloved

Forever My Earl

Always My Viscount

Infinitely My Marquess

EternallyMyDuke

Kismet Bay

Once Upon a Christmas

New Year Revelation

All Things Valentine

Luck At First Sight

Endless Summer Days

A Witch's Charm

All Out of Gratitude

Christmas Ever After

ACKNOWLEDGMENTS

This is where I thank my editor and cover artist, Victoria Miller profusely. She helps me more than I can ever say. I appreciate everything she does and that she pushes me to be better...do better. Thank you a thousand times over.

Also to Elizabeth Evans. Thank you for always being there for me and being my friend. You mean so much to me. Thanks isn't nearly enough, but it's all I have, so thank you my friend for being you.

AUTHOR'S NOTE

For all my readers that love the Linked Across Time series. The last few books mean even more than I can say. I hope you enjoy them the end, and look forward to a new adventure, and new series to come, including a spinoff series titled Scandalous Gentlemen coming in 2021.